Discipleship

For

Student

Athletes

Practical Insights for Discipling Student Athletes

Dr. Ed Gomes

In the process of developing a website to download free power point lessons and to contact Ed Gomes, at www.edgomes.com

Dedication

Discipleship for Student Athletes is dedicated to the
Student-Athletes who were a part of the discipleship
experience we had together.

Introduction

It is encouraging to see how sports continue to be used as a platform to teach character and spiritual values to athletes today. On the other hand, we must be aware that there are some who use sports as a tool to teach things that are based only on a temporal value system. *Discipling for Student Athletes* is based on an eternal value system and philosophy that is rooted in God's Word.

The Whole Person Development approach seeks to use athletics as a platform to teach character and spiritual values that are established on an eternal value system. This system gives attention to the four major areas (Academic, Athletic, Social and Spiritual) in the life of a student-athlete. It is a holistic approach for making disciples.

To illustrate the Whole Person Development model, visualize yourself planning to make a long trip with your family. One of the things you do before leaving for the trip is drop off your car at your auto mechanics shop to have a general maintenance checkup. While doing the checkup, the mechanic notices that the air pressure in a few of the tires is not where it needs to be. Some air is added to get the tires to their proper air pressure so that your ride will be more enjoyable.

Can you imagine the negative impact on your family enjoying the long ride across country because you don't have the right amount of pressure in each tire? Do you think that not having the right amount of air pressure could limit the gas mileage you would get per gallon of gas? Do you think the car may have a tendency to veer to one side of the road? Is it possible the tires may not wear evenly as you are travel down the highway? What a difference in the ride if you have the right amount of air pressure in each tire from the start of the trip!

The same thing is true for the student-athlete who embraces the Academic, Athletic, Social and Spiritual components of the Whole Person Development model. The outcome would be a more balanced life… It would be a life that adds value to the team. It would be transformational.

Discipleship for Student Athletes book provides questions and answers that will empower you to make an impact in the lives of student-athletes. You will discover some very practical ways in which you can develop spiritual leaders who will, in turn, transform the culture of the team.

Discipleship for Student Athletes book is designed to be a resource that compliments the *Leaving A Legacy* (Leaders and Coach's Guide) and *Building A Legacy* (Student Guide) discipleship manuals. They are discipleship lessons that can be used for one-on-one, small group, and team discipleship. The lessons are primarily geared towards everyday experiences that student-athletes encounter. May God use us to impact student athletes?

God bless, Ed Gomes

Table of Contents

Endorsements

"Ed Gomes has a passion and biblically based plan for discipleship of student-athletes that leads to spiritual growth and maturity. His practical insights and wealth of experience are clearly presented in *"Discipleship for Student-Athletes."*

__**Ian McCaw,**   Director of Athletics,   Liberty University

"This book is a must for any Christian coach, athletic department staff member or teacher who is truly in the profession for the right reasons. Dr. Gomes presents a clear guide on how to disciple student-athletes as they participate in your program and beyond. The principles of Whole Person Development are woven throughout the chapters and all the nuts and bolts for an effective discipleship ministry are included. I would highly recommend this book to serve as a blueprint to fully maximize on the unique platform coaches have to minister to student-athletes."

__**Frank A. Rocco,**   CAA,   Athletic Director/Head Coach,   Liberty Christian Academy

"Dr. Gomes has provided insight and discipleship to student-athletes for over 19 years. His passion and enthusiasm for sharing God's love with athletes, has been an extraordinary and an enriching experience. This book provides a holistic approach to discipling student-athletes in academic, athletic, social and spiritual principles which will truly influence their journey of life."

__**Dr. Vicky Martin,** Full Professor Department of Sport, Event & Tourism Management School of Business

"For years I have had the pleasure of seeing Ed Gomes and student-athletes spending time together. There are smiles and laughter, and each student knows that the man sitting across the table truly cares about him. One of the wonderful things about Ed's meetings is that he doesn't just "wing it." He has a goal and a well-reasoned way to achieve that goal. Before the meeting is over, Ed is going to encourage each student to never stop growing in his personal relationship with Christ, and he is going to help that student discover how to make his faith in Christ practical. Ed has studied well and has learned from decades of personal experience how to engage and lead the next generation of student athlete. So, grab your highlighter, your pen, and your notebook because you're going to want to take a lot of notes while reading this book!"

__**Allen Miller**, Area Director, Central Virginia Young Life

"In this book Dr. Ed Gomes lays out practical insight for developing champions for Christ. Ed hits a homerun as one of the best guides for someone who has the desire to reach their maximum potential throughout the seasons of life. This is a must read for anyone desiring to acquire a whole person development, or for leaders using it to guide others towards excellence. I personally found the section on "Time Management" in Chapter 5 to be my favorite. Of all the gifts that God has given us, the gift of TIME is the only one you can never get back, so we MUST make it count."

-**Rod Gladfelter,** Physical Education Teacher, Motivational Speaker and Former College Football Coach

"After twenty years of being the Campus Director of the Fellowship of Christian Athletes and Team Chaplin for the Football team at Auburn University, Dr. Ed Gomes has captured in this book the biblical principles we all have been waiting for - Young men and women can sit around for three to five years at their perspective school and never achieve what God wants - healthy relationships, a strong character, and freedom from their past. Or they can stop making excuses and learn how to deal with yesterday, so their future will be full of hope and good choices. Thanks Dr. Ed for a ground-breaking work on discipling athletes."

-**Chette Williams**,   FCA Campus Director and Football Chaplain, Auburn University

"Ed Gomes has a passion for student-athletes that elevates every person associated with him. Since 2004, I have had the privilege to learn about Whole Person Development. It challenged me as a young coach not to just focus on my student-athletes field production but to delve deeper in their lives - academically, socially, spiritually, as well as athletically. Applying the strategies that Ed Gomes taught our staff during my time at Liberty prepared me to be more than just a football coach. The Whole Person Development approach allowed me to build lasting relationships with former student-athletes that went deeper than a football career. I have been able to plant life - lesson seeds in these young men that helped mold them into great husbands, fathers, and men of character. This book will provide great insight to help you pour into your student-athletes and provide strategies to help these young men live life to the fullest."

-**Robert Wimberly**,   Northern Illinois Football, Executive Assistant Coach/Co-Def. Coordinator/LB

"*Discipleship for Student-Athletes* is chock-full of insightful yet practical tools for discipleship. Dr. Gomes is one of the leading experts in his field and lends his experience in sport ministry to the pages of this book. The fact that he's intentional in developing a strategic plan of discipleship toward athletes is a real blessing."

-**Dave Gittings**,   FCA Campus Sports Ministry and Football Chaplain, Virginia Tech

"Dr. Ed Gomes latest book, *Discipleship for Student-Athletes* unashamedly proclaims godly character development to be the central purpose of college athletics. He advocates that those called to lead student-athletes need to set their goals on eternal values and he provides biblical and personal insights on how to develop athletes in godliness and character development. Ed follows a wholistic approach to addressing the student's academic, athletic, social and spiritual life. This is a must read for all who seek to coach and lead with an eternal purpose."

-**Dr. Steven Keith**,   Director of Center for Chaplaincy, Liberty University

"*Discipleship for Student Athletes* is an invaluable tool for both athletic coaches and spiritual mentors. Dr. Gomes, from his years of experience as an athlete, coach and spiritual mentor, has shared invaluable principles to help us in our ministry of discipleship."

-**Dan Manley**,   Senior Pastor,   Lakewood Baptist Church

"The first moment I met Dr. Ed Gomes, I knew God's favor was on his life from our conversations because it was always about Christ and his goal to share the love of Christ

16

with others. Dr. Gomes's ability to articulate discipline is a part of developing young men spiritually on and off the field. Those experiences have given Ed Gomes the insight to produce a plan for developing the whole person with a focus centered on Christ first and character values. This book is a great guide for a better and blessed life. *Discipleship for Student Athletes* is a must read for all leaders.

Ed Vickers, Founder and CEO, ATAXES, LLC, Vancouver, WA and Former Liberty University Basketball Player and Inductee into Liberty University Athletics Hall of Fame

"When I reflect on my time at Liberty University, both as a student and an athlete, I cannot do so without thinking about how God used Ed Gomes to shape and transform my life. He is a model of love, intentionality, and godliness. His deep conviction to see Christ multiplied in every player, position group, and coach is evident in the lives of all who have gone through the Liberty football program. One thing I love about Ed is how he believes that success is not success without a successor as he is always putting 2 Timothy 2:2 into practice. Simple things grow. Simple things multiply. By the grace of God and as a testament to Gomes' I am a living example of his ministry. *Discipleship for Student Athletes* is a wonderful overflow of Ed Gomes life, experience, and legacy in book form, showing how to transform student-athlete's lives through meaningful and intentional discipleship relationships. I believe it will be both a blessing and a reproducing pattern that many will use in the years ahead."

Zach Duke, Former Wide Receiver JDA Worldwide

"*Discipleship for Student-Athletes* is an incredible tool for ministry. As someone who walked through this material with my mentor, know the life-changing effect it has on student-athletes. I am thankful for Ed and this book. It has had a profound influence on my development and I cannot wait to see how God uses it to change more lives."

-Javan Shashaty, Student Pastor, Calvary Chapel Fort Lauderdale Former Quarterback

"Dr. Gomes is a passionate leader who is deeply invested in the growth of the student-athletes at Liberty University and more specifically on its football team. He demonstrates leadership through his intent listening of student-athletes' up and down moments, both counseling and celebrating with them. He is valued for his wisdom and guidance developed over decades of spiritual leadership and investment in thousands of student-athletes. It was an honor to interact with and be counseled by Ed Gomes during my time at Liberty University. I trust that he continues to work diligently, improving the athletes lives one-by-one and the lives of those around the student-athletes at Liberty."

Grant Bowden, Former Punter The MITRE Cooperation

"*Discipleship for Student-Athletes* is a practical tool for coaches, mentors and all others that have the opportunity to do life with student-athletes. While I played football at Liberty University, Ed Gomes used the practices and principles in this book to disciple many of my teammates and me. It not only trained us to be student-athletes that lived a balanced life using the Whole Person Development model it also taught us how to lead our peers and our future wives spiritually. This book will bear fruit long after athletic careers are complete, enabling student-athletes to be salt and light in their future homes, jobs and communities."

Miles Hunter, Student Pastor, Treasure Coast Community Church Former Linebacker

"*Discipleship for Student-Athletes* is a tool for mentors, coaches, and leaders to help empower student-athletes to reach their full potential in athletics and in life. Ed Gomes implementation of the Whole Person Development model has changed many lives by helping student-athletes understand the power of a firm foundation in all areas of life during college years. This book will encourage and inspire all who read to truly engage in discipleship, so that student-athletes can grow to be men and women who follow Christ."

Trey Turner, Former Punter Ronald Blue Trust

"*Discipleship for Student-Athletes*" is a book that I've personally seen lived out by my good friend and mentor, Dr. Ed Gomes. During my days as a collegiate athlete, he modeled the principles in this book as he poured into me weekly. The content and values in these pages will give you great insight on discipling student athletes with excellence. If you want to assist and encourage student-athletes to grow in their walks with Jesus, this is the book to read."

Cory Freeman, Student Pastor, Harvest Indy South Former Linebacker

Chapter One

Why Should Student-Athletes Be Discipled?

Just think what could happen if we invest our time, expertise and everyday life experiences in the lives of a student-athletes? The answer is very easy, a life will be impacted not only now, but for years to come. If that isn't a good enough reason, something is wrong.

The Biblical Mandate to Make Disciples

While reading the New Testament, it becomes very clear that the Master Teacher is very explicit about His instructions to make disciples. Sometimes the emphasis is placed more on evangelism than on making disciples. Don't get me wrong, evangelism is very important, but the primary weight in looking at the grammar in Matthew 28:19-20 is on making disciples. The Master Teacher not only communicated the command verbally, but He demonstrated it by the way He lived, the way He invested His time, prayer and life in others.

You may be asking why it is important to have a biblical mandate for making disciples? It is important because to have anything short of the biblical mandate, one cannot expect to have God's favor on the process used for making disciples.

Billie Hanks writes, *"The process of discipleship and discipleship making begins with a vision. We have to see, first of all, that discipleship represents the quality of life God expects of us as Christians. We are called to be followers of Jesus Christ – His disciples. But we are also mandated to "go and make disciples, and multiply."* 1

In other words, its foundation is not solid. It will not stand the test of time and authenticity. That process has a temporary manifestation, whereas a solid foundation that is biblical has a lasting and eternal manifestation. That's why it's important to follow the biblical mandate for discipling athletes.

The Need to Make Disciples

If there has ever been a time in athletics when a need to disciple student-athletes is needed, it is today. There is such a microwave or instant approach to everything. Nobody wants to wait. Everybody wants it now. Notice when you go shopping, how many varieties of foods you can purchase that you can put in the microwave and eat in a matter of minutes. I am not saying that is all bad, but when it comes to discipling student-athletes, it doesn't happen that way. It takes time, prayer, faithfulness and hard work to meet the needs of discipling. It doesn't make a difference what the profession is; today, there is a need for dependable and faithful people to help meet the spiritual needs of others.

That is also true when it comes to the subject of discipling student-athletes. What an opportunity we have to pour into the lives of players and in turn, they take what has been passed on to them and they make disciples. As one studies the life and ministry of the apostle Paul, you will realize very quickly that he was not only committed to evangelism alone but was very interested is seeing others grow in their faith and become true disciples of Christ. Yes, He was committed to evangelism everywhere He went and with whom He was with, but spiritual maturity *(Acts 15:36)* was also important to Him, as well. Sounds to me like a pretty good combination.

21

Do you see the need for discipling athletes? Will you let God use you to meet the challenge of making disciples amongst your players?

It's the Best Way to Develop Spiritual Leaders

The debate at times seems to focus on the following question: are leaders born leaders or are leaders developed? I believe that certain leadership qualities are given from God at the moment of birth; however, they need to be developed in order to maximize the effectiveness in leading others. The same is true when it comes to developing student-athletes as spiritual leaders. The sacrifice, effort, prayer and life-on-life time together is a possible way to develop spiritual-minded leaders, who will emerge as the spiritual leaders on the team. It's taking spiritual truth and passing it on to student-athletes who will in turn take those biblical and life principles and pass them on to other teammates, therefore developing spiritual leaders who can lead others. That is what Paul talks about in II Timothy 2:2.

Tony Dungy says, *"Mentor leadership focuses on building people up, building significance into their lives, and building leaders for the next generation."* 2

The method that Paul describes in the verse will certainly be a way to produce the leader's that are needed in all walks of life, and especially when it comes to growing spiritual leaders on an athletic team. There are no shortcuts for developing spiritual leaders on any team.

The Opportunity to Share Life Together is Enhanced

When you think of a student-athlete meeting with a spiritual mentor for spiritual growth, God does something during that time together. I have always viewed my meetings with players as a Life-on-Life opportunity - an opportunity to share life together with an athlete for edification and accountability. The things that a mentor shares with a mentee can be life changing. Occasionally during the discipleship time together, the mentor can share personal life experiences that can be very encouraging to the student-athlete. When we make ourselves available for God to use us that is exactly what he does.

I heard someone say during a conference, *"A message prepared in the mind reaches minds, a message prepared in the heart reaches hearts, but a message prepared in the life reaches and changes lives."* 3

Some of those life experiences have to do with salvation, spiritual development or even personal struggles. God allows us to have conversations with players, so they become opportunities to talk and look at life from God's perspective. Inter-connections of life, which God has allowed to happen for transformation, are sometimes called divine appointments. It's during those moments that God can bring about salvation, sanctification and character development in the life of athletes and others.

To Properly Prepare for the Numerical Growth of Spiritual-Minded Athletes

Is it normal to assume and believe there will be fruit from the joy of making disciples? The answer to that assumption is yes; there will be fruit. When a person plants potatoes, is it normal to expect a harvest of potatoes? Sure, it is, and the same thing is true of discipling student-athletes. Knowing that one of the by-products of discipling athletes is the growing number of student-athletes being discipled; therefore, you will be better prepared to respond to the numerical growth of leaders. Reproduction and multiplication are a normal expectancy when it comes to discpling student athletes. Failure to prepare for the growth of making disciples will hamper the ability to meet the growing demands of both the physical and spiritual needs of those being ministered to on the team. The more disciples you develop, the better prepared you are for continuing the work of the ministry among athletes.

Martin Sanders writes, "*New leaders need to be ready when the time comes for them to stand on the mountain, in the arena, in the university or wherever God has called them to stand. They need the heart, passion, strength and experiential base of a modern-day Elijah – to risk faith with the confidence and assurance that God is with them, to stand and make a difference for the generation after them.*" 4

When thinking about developing spiritual leaders for the future, it's important that your motives be genuine. Motive has to do with the following questions: Why am I doing what I am doing and who am I doing it for? Is it to please others (Gal. 1:10) or is it to please God? If it is for others it will be as the Bible says - wood, hay and straw. On the other hand, if it is being done to honor God and build up the kingdom, then it will be gold, silver and precious stone according to I Corinthians 3:12-13. Great questions to ponder as you think about those you are discipling. Let's continue to make disciples because it will help us to impact more student-athletes for His glory and not for anything else.

To Encourage Continual Progress Toward Spiritual Maturity

When you do a study of the life of Saul, who later became Paul, there are three different stages in his life journey that have application for today as we minister to athletes. Those stages are as follows. The first stage I have called the *Pre-Conversion Stage.* This is his life before salvation. It's about who he was. The second stage is called the *Conversion Stage.* This is his life at conversion. It's about who he became. The third stage is called the *Post-Conversion Stage.* This is his life after conversion. It's about who he was becoming. Paul mentions a variety of different types of people in the early chapters of the book I Corinthians. Some of the names he uses to describe the people written about were called the natural, spiritual, carnal and baby person. The point to be made is that making disciples is one of the greatest ways to assure spiritual maturity in the lives of student-athletes.

Gary Kuhue has the following to say about maturity, *"A person becomes a disciple when he becomes stabilized in the faith, has an ongoing commitment to the lordship of Christ, and had developed the basic disciplines of Christian living and service so that the lifelong maturing process is guaranteed, at least as much as is humanly possible."*5

Why Should Student-Athletes Be Discipled?

> ➤ *The Biblical Mandate to Make Disciples*
> ➤ *The Need to Make Disciples*
> ➤ *It's the Best Way to Develop Spiritual Leaders*
> ➤ *The Opportunity to Share Life Together is Enhanced*

> ➤ *To Properly Prepare for the Numerical Growth of Spiritual-Minded Athletes*
> ➤ *To Encourage Continual Progress Toward Spiritual Maturity*

Some Things to Ponder:

> ➤ *What Was One Thing I Learned from Reading the Chapter?*
> ➤ *How Will I Apply the One Thing I Have Learned from Reading the Chapter?*

Chapter Two

When Should Student-Athletes Be Discipled?

Have you ever observed a student-athlete and then ask yourself the following question: I wonder if the student-athlete needs to talk to someone about something?

During the Ordinary Events of Life

Some of those ordinary events could take place while the athlete is participating in the sport and other times it could be away from the sporting event or practice. There are many possible places where conversations can take place with student-athletes in the locker room, practice field, cafeteria, dormitory, restaurant, office and a plethora of other settings to only name a few. Occasionally the conversations center around a career-ending injury, a death in the family, a mistake made while in competition, spiritual setback, breakup with a girlfriend or boyfriend, academic failure, and a host of other possibilities that provide opportunities to talk with student athletes.

Bruce Wilkerson writes, *"We hear God's rebuke even though we don't always choose to respond. God can make Himself heard in many ways: a prick of our conscience, a timely word from another person, a Scripture, the preaching of the Word or conviction by the Holy Spirit."* 1

There are times when God may allow us to see something, hear something or experience something with purpose. There are some who would say that we are to always confront when we see, hear or experience something that may not be wholesome. I would like to suggest a few things. The first suggestion would be to pray about the matter. Prayer causes us to look at life from God's perspective. It also allows us to think through what we may say or do before we say or do something that may not be helpful to the situation. Secondly, maybe it was one of those times in life that we would categorize as a bad moment. Anybody can have a bad moment. Now if what you see, hear or experience is a pattern, then you may want to speak to the person out of love and concern. It could be a blind spot in the life of the individual. The good thing about your conversation is it would have been bathed in prayer and the leading of the Holy Spirit. Thirdly, God may want you to just leave it alone and learn a valuable lesson for yourself on what not to do if you find yourself in a similar situation. The bottom line is depend on God for wisdom and biblical insight to properly respond to everyday life situations that you may see, hear or experience.

When a Student-Athlete Asks a Question

As we make ourselves available for God to use us, that's exactly what He does. Sometimes He will allow us to have a conversation with an athlete and during the conversation we may be asked a question that may not have anything to do with the spiritual matters but does provide an open door to talk about life in general. The question could be related to a computer or an automobile problem the player may be having. On the other hand, there are times when we will be asked a question that is spiritual in nature. It's important for each of us to be good listeners because there will be times when one question will open a door to discuss something that may be spiritual. The more attentive and engaged we are during the conversation, we can better answer the question we are being asked. I am reminded of a biblical example in the Old Testament of someone who was attentive and observant while in prison. You may remember the story of Joseph while he was in prison. During that experience, there were two men who had dreams but didn't know what the dreams meant. Joseph was able to provide them an answer for the experiences they did not understand. He was able to help them interpret their dreams, even though it was good news for one and for the other it was bad news. In other words, one was going to have his position restored and the other was going to have his head taken off. Let's be good listeners because there will be times when athletes will come and ask questions and we want to be like Joseph in providing possible answers to their life's inquiries.

Whenever a Teachable Moment Presents Itself

Teachable moments show up at times when we least expect them to surface. As we study the life and ministry of our Master Teacher, we will see many examples of Jesus using the everyday situations with his disciples and others He encountered. Not only did He use teachable moments with His disciples, but with the religious leaders and many others He met during his earthly ministry. Teachable moments provide an opportunity to build genuine relationships with people. It is amazing when we properly respond to people God is trying to use to shape and mold us into the image of Christ: that's exactly what he does. Now it may be a little awkward, but after the process is over we become more like Christ in our attitudes and actions, therefore reflecting Christlikeness.

Dennis Maynard writes, *"Learning to discern the presence of the spiritual begins by understanding that spirituality manifests itself in a broad context of life experiences, not merely in religious experiences."* 2

Many times, teachable moments with our athletes provide an opportunity to live out what we preach and teach to our athletes. For some of us, it could mean living out our athletic vision, mission and core values in front of our players. It is refreshing for players to see coaches and support staff living out what is being taught within the athletic program.

When a Student-Athlete Requests a Meeting

There will be times when an athlete will reach out to speak with someone. It could be a coach, professor, teammate or a spiritual advisor. The circumstances may be different each time the athlete reaches out, but it will happen. Everybody in life must reach out to somebody to help sort out life at one point or another. Athletes are no different than anyone else. As we continue to make ourselves available for God to use, that is what He does. What an honor to have a student-athlete come and speak to us about whatever may be on his or her mind. When that happens, we need to be good listeners and be sure to ask good questions that will provide sound wisdom from a biblical perspective.

A good example of this is seen in the temple when Jesus was just twelve years old in Luke 2:46-50. Some have called those kind of meetings divine appointments. They sometime take place when we don't expect them: therefore, we must seek to help others properly interpret life issue's God's way. What an honor to speak truth into the lives of coaches and athletes as we serve them.

After a Student-Athlete Has Experienced Failure or Made a Mistake

We don't go around like police officers looking for athletes making bad choices: however, every so often something will come our way that reflects the sport we are participating in at that time in a negative way. These kinds of scenarios provide an opportunity to demonstrate the motives for what we do and who we serve. There are times when God may use a person or situation to bring about change in the life of the student-athlete. God uses all kinds of people and life experiences to help an athlete evaluate where he or she is in relationship with God. There are times God when God will use people and situations to lead a person to Christ. Other times God maybe using people and situations to help a person become more like Christ or to develop character in the life of the individual.

There are two choices for the players. One is to *react* and then life gets more complicated. The following characteristics could indicate the student-athlete is reacting: one defends self, holds things in, blames others, lives in a dream world, and makes excuses, etc. Two, is to *respond* to what God is trying to do through the person and situation. The following characteristics could indicate that the player is responding: takes full responsibility for what has happened, is willing to face the consequences for what has taken place, and willing to make restitution if necessary. Finally, the athlete is willing to ask the following questions: What can I learn about God through the person or situation? What can I learn about

31

myself through the person or situation? What can I learn about the person through the situation? What character qualities can I apply to the situation? What is the best method to use to communicate, if possible?

Reacting would be the devil's way of dealing with the person or situation. Responding would be God's way of dealing with the person or situation. The conversation is an opportunity to express your thoughts regarding the situation, but also to affirm your love for the student-athlete during a very difficult time in his/her life.

During the Loss of Family Member, Close Friend or Personal Injury

During a time of loss or injury we have a great opportunity to serve those we are working with daily. That is a time for us to make ourselves available to be a source of encouragement during the unexpected loss. We may have a chance to share something from the Word or just have a word of prayer. Simply practicing the ministry of presence can be a blessing to the player or family. Other times it may mean that we will make a phone call, send a card or use some other form of communication through social media to communicate our love and concern during the tough time.

Sometimes we can talk to the player or family member about where they spiritually are at that moment. It can be a chance to share the hope we have in Christ and maybe even a chance to talk about how to grow spiritually through the tragedy. It is not only good to be there when things are going well, but when things are not going well for the athlete. Real friends are there all the time regardless of what is going on in the life of the student-athlete. One of the things we see in the life and ministry of Jesus is that Jesus always showed up at the right time to meet the needs of those He was ministering with and to. It is always good to be available when there is a need because God may want to use us to be a blessing to someone in time of need.

When Should Student-Athletes Be Discipled?

> *During the Ordinary Events of Life*
> *When a Student-Athlete Asks a Question*
> *Whenever a Teachable Moment Presents Itself*
> *When a Student-Athlete Requests a Meeting*
> *After a Student-Athlete Has Experienced Failure or Made a Mistake*
> *During the Loss of Family Member, Close Friend or Personal Injury*

Some Things to Ponder:

> *What Was One Thing I Learned from Reading the Chapter?*
> *How Will I Apply the One Thing I Have Learned from Reading the Chapter?*

Chapter Three

Where Should Student-Athletes Be Discipled?

Do you recall having a conversation with a student-athlete and knew right away why you were meant to have that conversation? God allows those kinds of interactions to happen, so we may share some words of life, or just be a good listener at the moment.

During a One-on-One or Small Group Meeting

Trying to determine the best place for discipleship is often designated by those who are being discipled. There are times when discipleship is done one-on-one and other times when more than one athlete is present. I have the opportunity to meet with our players ranging from one player to as many as four players in a discipleship gathering. I try to limit the group to no more than four players for weekly discipleship meetings. When scheduling the discipleship meetings at the outset, I will ask the student athlete if he prefers a one-on-one discipleship meeting or would he mind joining other teammates. The one-on-one meeting is best, especially if there is something personal in nature that the athlete needs to talk about. I also assure players who are in a group setting if they ever need to talk with me about something personal outside the meeting, they can always feel free to let me know and I will set up the one-on-one time with them. It has been my experience that after the athlete feels comfortable in the one-on-one meeting, he is a little more open to joining a group for discipleship.

Dave Early pens, *"Involvement in small group life and leadership was a primary spiritual discipline in the life of Jesus Christ. Following Jesus today means following Him in deep relationships with other believers His pattern was gathering a few to transform the many."*

Whenever I am meeting with more than one player for discipleship and other players desire to join the group, I always tell them that I will think about it and get back with them in a reasonable time. I then talk with the players in the group first and then follow up with those interested in my final decision. I don't reveal who is in that group unless I am asked. I have never had anybody say they didn't want another teammate to join their group. As you can see, each discipleship meeting develops its own personality and we must respect its identity and wishes of the group. If someone in the group doesn't want the player to join the group, I then seek dialogue with that person who objects and then together with other players in the group. Once you have had honest and thorough discussion, then you as the leader make your decision. It is good to inform the athletes in the group first and then inform the player seeking to join the group afterward.

In the Most Convenient Place

In attempting to locate the most convenient place to have a discipleship meeting, you must assess the need of the moment and look to find a place that will help create the most favorable environment for all involved. Sometimes it may be on the practice field, a nearby park, cafeteria, bookstore, your office, or even somewhere on campus. You want the place to have privacy. It is also good to vary the place where you meet for. Occasionally having a meeting outside is a nice change of setting for discipleship. Being creative about where you have your meetings is always a good thing as well.

During an Unexpected Experience in Life

Maybe you have had one of your athletes ask to speak with you because something may need to be brought to the attention of the head coach. Some of those unexpected experiences might include, pregnancy, tragedy, arrest, bad news from home and a host of other possibilities. If something is brought to your attention that you think the head coach needs to be made aware of, it is wise to ask God for wisdom in your dialogue with the athlete. You may have to let the player know that you will have to inform the head coach about what happened, or you can ask the player to speak with the coach. You can even offer to go with the student athlete to speak to the head coach about the matter. It is very important for the head coach to not get blindsided by someone or something that has taken place outside the athletic program. It is worth mentioning that there are some things that don't need to go to the head coach, it may just need to be shared with an assistant coach. In some cases, I may bring it to the attention of the coordinator, as well. Remember, if you are going to share any information with the coaching staff make sure you talk with the player first because of the importance of confidentiality, therefore not hindering the relationship with you and the player.

David Stoddard rightfully states, *"What people need most is a listening heart, an understanding look, perhaps a gentle, reassuring touch, and words sparingly."* 2

Generally, if the information could affect the team in a negative manner, you should ask God for wisdom and have good dialogue with the player about what needs to be shared with the head coach. It is always about doing the right thing. Sometimes the burden weighs heavy on the player and you are the one person who can give the student-athlete the proper guidance during that very difficult time.

In the Presence of Another Person

There are times when it is good to have somebody with you when you are meeting with a player. One reason is to provide a different perspective on the subject you are about to discuss with the athlete. Having additional counsel provides a chance to evaluate how the meeting went. You can ask each other questions about what was said or not said during the meeting. This type of scenario doesn't happen often in a discipleship meeting; however, it is good to keep it in mind especially if you must deal with a discipline issue or failure in the life of the student-athlete. While one person is talking, the other person is listening and praying that God would give wisdom and discernment during the meeting.

Tim Elmore shares, *"There is no life-change without life-exchange."* 3

Where the Conversation Will Not Be Interrupted

It should be a place where each person is able to talk openly and honestly with each other without any interruptions. Interruptions have a way of breaking the chain of thought and important discussion with each other. During a discipleship meeting in my office, it is my policy to only answer the phone (office or cell) if it is my wife or the head coach seeking to talk with me. After the meeting I will follow up with the person who called. Creating an un-interrupted meeting allows the student-athlete to know that the meeting is important and his/her time is valued.

In a Casual or Structured Setting

The settings for discipleship may differ according to the need. Maybe you have been asked the following questions a time or two: Do I always need to use a book for my discipleship with athletes? Do my discipleship meetings need to be structured or have a little freedom to let the meetings take on their own uniqueness? Those are good questions that demand a good response. The answers to those questions have to do with what the need of the athlete is you are discipling. For some it may mean that you are going to begin the discipleship process with some practical and biblical insights that you would consider to be foundational in your discipleship ministry, and then move into a possible book study that will address the specific needs of the athlete.

One of our student-athletes asked me the following question: Can we just have discussions about life when we meet for our weekly meeting? That was a great question. When discipling our student athletes, I use a discipleship book I have developed titled *Building A Legacy*. It is my primary discipleship resource with our players. My initial answer to the question was no. After a few days I began to ask myself how did Jesus do it? I concluded that there were times Jesus had a formal setting with His disciples and at other times it was just determined by the moment and need. Well, after thinking about the question, I told the athlete we would alternate picking a lesson from the discipleship book and every other week we would just have a conversation about anything we wanted to talk about. There are several lessons learned from the question and the response. It is healthy for the disciple to be able to ask discipler questions about the process of discipleship. Secondly, it is good to be flexible in what is being used for discipleship. Thirdly, good relationships are developed through open and honest dialogue between the disciple and the discipler. It is important to be flexible in determining what you use for discipling your athletes.

Where Should Student-Athletes Be Discipled?

> *During a One-on-One or Small Group Meeting*
> *In the Most Convenient Place*
> *During an Unexpected Experience in Life*
> *In the Presence of Another Person*
> *Where the Conversation Will Not Be Interrupted*
> *In a Casual or Structured Setting*

Some Things to Ponder:

> *What Was One Thing I Learned from Reading the Chapter?*
> *How Will I Apply the One Thing I Have Learned from Reading the Chapter?*

Chapter Four

How Should Student-Athletes Be Discipled?

Have you ever had an encounter with a student-athlete that caught you off guard, and had to utilize the moment to say and do what met the need?

According to Need

Student-athletes, at different times during and after the season, will develop a variety of needs that require attention. These needs could be academic, athletic, social and spiritual, and it is important to have resources and people in place to meet these needs as they arise. Each of us have primary responsibilities, however, we may have to minister outside our primary area. For example, I may talk to an athlete about his academic life and realize he has a subject that requires attention in a certain subject matter. Even though academics is not my primary area of responsibility, I know is very important, Therefore, I make sure he gets help in that area of his life.

Faithfully and Lovingly Way

Many times, discussions focus on what it means to be successful in life. That is a good question that needs frequent exploration. I am all for success, however, when I am asked about being successful, I like to remind people it is more about being faithful in your relationship with God, your relationship with your family, and in your work or ministry. In other words, put God first, family second, and work and ministry third. To get priorities out of balance means someone will receive a negative impact. We are reminded in I

40

Corinthians 4:1-2 to be faithful stewards of God. As stewards we must be found faithful where we are planted and trust God for His results. I believe it is possible to be successful while being faithful in doing the work of the ministry. While being faithful in serving where God has placed us, let us remember our love for God and others is what motivates us to be faithful where we are planted. As stewards of God, we can serve students and others with passion and pleasure because our motives rest on expressing the love of God through our attitudes and actions.

Through Clearly Communicated Expectations

When expectations are clearly communicated it is easier to understand what is expected from each person involved in the discipleship process. Hopefully, in the first discipleship meeting you can clearly communicate what the expectations will be for each other or for your small group. The expectations have to do with when you will meet, the place you will meet, the time you will meet, what happens when you cannot meet because of circumstances beyond your control, and what the format will be when you meet.

Joel Manby writes, *"Don't assume other people see what you see. Put it on the table."* 1

Included could be what you study together and how to follow the format. When expectations are clearly expressed, you set a standard by which to evaluate the progress of your discipleship time together. In other words, do not merely meet, meet with a purpose.

With Dependence on God, God's Word, and Guidance of the Holy Spirit

To effectively impact student-athletes in all areas of whole-person development, we need to have total dependence on God and have a value system based on the Word of God at our core. In God's Word, we can distinguish between right and wrong. The Word becomes our standard for developing a better understanding of who He is and how He works in everyday life experiences.

Tim Clinton writes, *"God has given us everything we need for success in this life, but be sure you read the bold declarations appearing throughout his word: action required."* 2

Not only do we need to depend on God and the blueprint He has given us in the Bible, but we need to rely on the Holy Spirit to guide us as we minister. A dependence on the Holy Spirit allows us to see and hear things during our dialogue with student-athletes. It is during those times that we learn to discern His will while engaged in the ministry of discipleship.

Utilizing a Systematic Plan for Developing Spiritual Maturity

When you think of the process an infant goes through, from dependence on the mother for sustenance to being able to feed itself, the same is true for a spiritual baby. Physical and spiritual growth does not happen automatically. As a process exists that allows a person to move through the physical stages of life, the same is true with spiritual growth.

Chris Adsit shares in his book titled, Personal Discipleship-Making, *"We need to see ourselves primarily as the "earthly instruments" God uses to facilitate the maturing process of His children." 3*

To help student-athletes grow spiritually there needs to be a plan in place to see maturity become a reality. The student-athletes I work with daily use something I put together called *Building A Legacy*. In the *Building A Legacy* discipleship manual, there are over one hundred and five lessons that relate primarily to the life experiences of student-athletes. There are many other materials that can be used for discipling athletes and I use other materials depending on the need, but my primary source for discipleship is *Building A Legacy*.

In One-On-One or Small Group Meetings

Various opportunities exist to disciple student-athletes as it relates to the size of the group. I have discipleship meetings that consist of one to four players, not including myself. While there are numerous materials for discipleship with student-athletes, the primary materials I use with our athletes come from my *Building A Legacy* discipleship manual. During discipleship meetings, regardless the size of the group, the individual who picks the lesson gets to ask anyone in the group one general question about anything in life. This general question does not have to relate to the lesson to be studied together. The following week is about asking or discussing whatever is on the mind of those in the group. Picking a lesson one week and the following week having dialogue is the way I lead the discipleship meetings, regardless of the size of the group. These discipleship meetings provide a tremendous opportunity to speak truth into the lives of those being discipled. It is amazing how this method of study encourages each player to open up and contribute to the discussion during the discipleship meetings.

How Should Student-Athletes Be Discipled?

- ➤ *According to Need*
- ➤ *Faithful and Lovingly*
- ➤ *Through Clearly Communicated Expectations*
- ➤ *With Dependence on God, God's Word, and Guidance of The Holy Spirit*
- ➤ *Utilizing a Systematic Plan for Developing Spiritual Maturity*
- ➤ *Through One-on-One or Small Group Meetings*

Some Things to Ponder:

- ➤ *What Was One Thing I Learned from Reading the Chapter?*
- ➤ *How Will I Apply the One Thing I Have Learned from Reading the Chapter?*

Chapter Five

What Areas Should Student-Athletes Be Disciple In?

When is the last time you engaged in a conversation with a student-athlete and very quickly knew the direction the dialogue needed to go?

How to Incorporate Spiritual Disciplines in Everyday Life

One of the greatest and most important areas a student-athlete develops in their spiritual walk has to do with spiritual disciplines. Spiritual disciplines are the basics for developing a growing relationship with God. They lay the foundation for building a healthy spiritual walk before God and others. Some spiritual disciplines are: Bible study, prayer, daily devotions, journaling, and praise music memorizing scripture, meditation, and solitude.

Patrick Morley writes, *"Disciplines are the spiritual habits by which we cultivate deeper walk with the Lord of heaven and earth"* 1

Spiritual disciplines help formulate the core values and life-changing principles for a student-athlete to build and develop a life upon. They help an athlete move through the normal stages of spiritual growth from spiritual infancy to spiritual maturity.

How to Overcome Temptation

Regardless of where one is in their walk with God, the enemy's game plan never changes. He desires to get every student-athlete out of position in their vertical and horizontal relationships. It is crucial to help student-athletes develop a game plan for dealing with and overcoming temptation early in life, because temptation does not go away with age.

Terry Wardle says, *"Satan constantly works to lead people into bondage and ultimate eternal destruction."* 2

As we spend time discipling athletes we can help them utilize principles from athletics that apply to their spiritual lives. There are many principles and character qualities from athletics that can be incorporated into the spiritual journey of student-athletes, therefore becoming an overcomer.

How to Manage Time

One of the consistent needs I hear from our student-athletes is how to manage their time properly. During any given day, student-athletes are constantly on the move fulfilling the various obligations they have as students. Moving from one event to another can be demanding when it comes to using time correctly. As student-athletes learn how to use and manage their time, they enjoy a better college life. Part of learning to manage their time well has to do with setting respectable priorities during the day and week. As athletes learn how to grow in this area, they will develop habits that benefit them in years to come.

How to Live a Life of Servant Leadership

In studying the life of our Master Teacher, Jesus, one of His greatest qualities demonstrated was servant-leadership. He preached it, lived it, and demonstrated it all the way to the cross. One of the highest qualities our athletes can live out before their teammates is servant-leadership. Learning to focus on others and not on self is a great way to live every day. It also is one of the best ways for athletes to earn the right to be heard. The sport athletes participate in become the training ground for bigger and better things to come; as they learn to serve others. One good thing about making servant-leadership a way of life is that it takes the focus off the athlete and puts the focus on others. We are at our best when we help others succeed in life.

How to Build Healthy Relationships

The highest relationship we can help our athletes develop is their relationship with God. As the athlete grows in that relationship it will impact all other relationships. Some of those other relationships are with family, friends, teammates and girlfriends or boyfriends. The ability to relate to others becomes an important part of discipleship, because when the athlete finishes competing in athletics, hopefully will have learned how to relate to others under different circumstances.

Jon Gordon says, *"When you encourage each other, you make one another stronger and you make the team stronger."* 3

Athletics is a great tool to help athletes learn how to work together as a team. The opportunity to learn about self-discipline, self-motivation, setting goals, following instructions in disagreement are only a few way's athletics prepare an athlete for life after the sport. As the athlete learns how to maintain their vertical relationship; with God, that relationship will have a positive impact upon the horizontal relationships with people.

How to Develop Spiritual and Natural Leadership

One awesome opportunity we have is to help student-athletes utilize their God-given abilities and gifts to impact others through leadership development. Sometimes it is easier to see leadership potential in a player than it is for the player to see it in themselves. Ministry opportunities within sports provide tremendous avenues for student-athletes to demonstrate leadership qualities. As God allows us to develop spiritual leaders on the teams we serve, it is through discipleship we instruct, encourage, and exhort our athletes to cultivate a leadership lifestyle. The lifestyle benefits all areas of whole-person development. What a joy it is to see players apply leadership in all those areas. Keep in mind, while some spiritual and natural gifts in leadership surface immediately, others develop in time. During the discipleship process opportunities will arise through every day experiences to show athletes where they can and should use their leadership skills to impact others. I think it is important to help athletes understand that leadership begins by leading themselves first, and afterward they can begin to lead others.

John Maxwell is point on when he says, *"The first person you must lead will always be you. If you want to see positive change in your world, the first person you must change is you. As leaders, you and I have to be changed to bring change. We teach what we know, but we produce who we are."* 4

When it comes to leadership, one of the first things a student-athlete can learn is to lead himself or herself in all areas of whole-person development. The best way an athlete can influence another is to demonstrate leadership in their personal life. This is called leading by example. No one can

48

argue with someone who sets an example for others to follow. The greatest example set by a person who lived on earth is our Master Teacher, Jesus. We witnessed His leadership in the temple when He was twelve years old, and we saw it lived out in His life and ministry. Another person who modeled leadership was my Mother. She would say to us on numerous occasions, "Don't just do as I say, but do as I do." Mother was telling us that she would lead by example in attitude and actions. That was how she consistently modeled leadership in front of all eleven of her children. That is the same way we should model it in front of our student athletes, and they, in turn should model it in front of their teammates. That is real leadership.

How to Share a Personal Testimony and Present the Gospel

The occasion for a player to share their testimony with a fellow athlete is important. It is significant because God allows teammates to develop relationships over time. During the development of these relationships and conversations, God can use a student-athlete's testimony to lead another teammate to salvation or to a greater desire to walk with God. Knowing how to present an impromptu personal testimony of salvation or talk about spiritual growth is one way to use the sports platform to honor and glorify God. Many times, teammates do not mention how another player's walk with God has been instrumental in their personal growth or consideration of salvation. An athlete available to be used by God to impact another athlete spiritually, puts himself or herself in a place where God can use them to influence other teammates.

Not only is it important for an athlete to share a personal testimony, but we must teach athletes how to share the gospel in a practical and logical sequence. One blessing of being on a team is that you get the opportunity to develop relationships with other players. Those relationships allow athletes to share the gospel in a natural setting and provide opportunities for athletes to share with teammates how God is at work in their lives on a daily lives. What a privilege to teach student-athletes how to weave a personal testimony into a gospel presentation with another teammate.

How to Understand My Identity in Christ

For athletes to understand their identity in Christ is paramount; because their identity often gets wrapped up in their athletic performance. But performance-based identity is the exact opposite of the identity considered a gift. Salvation is a gift from God. There is nothing an athlete can do to earn it, purchase it, or work for it. It is a gift, period. We are saved by grace and grace alone according to Ephesians 2:8-9. What Christ provided for us by His sacrifice was accepted by our heavenly Father as a payment for our sin debt according to II Corinthians 5:21. Do not get me wrong, what a player does as an athlete is significant, however, it is not the most important thing they do.

Kenneth Boa writes, *"Exchanged life spiritually concentrates on the reality of a new identity through the in-Christ relationship that can dramatically transform us as we progressively grasp it in our experience."5*

An athlete's identity has to do with whom the athlete is in Christ. Knowing whom they are in Christ is about viewing themselves from God's perspective. Their identity is primarily about being, and not doing. It is all about understanding whom the athlete is in Christ. Their true identity is the foundation for everything else done through athletics. So; when an athlete makes a mistake in the game of life or in athletics, the athlete can remember that regardless of want happens, I am a child of God. When athletes remember who they are in Christ, they can respond to whatever happens in life, or in the sport they participate in from a biblical perspective. Yes, it is okay to feel bad about having a career ending injury, however, as you process the situation, you can view what has happened with the idea of whom you are in Christ and not by what you do as an athlete. It is the Rock on which you build your life upon. That foundation is secure and safe; because it is on the Rock which is Christ.

How to Disciple Another Teammate

The ability to help another teammate grow in Christ, is, in my opinion a great mark of spiritual maturity. Discipleship might begin with a teammate who has just received Christ as their personal Savior. Some call that "follow-up" after conversion. What a joy to be able to nurture a new believer in Christ. It is amazing to see how God, through consistent fellowship, study of the Word, and application from the Word to daily life, allows a person to grow in faith. In I Corinthians chapters two and three we find Paul describing four types of people natural, baby, carnal and spiritual. Each person cited has characteristics that identify who they are by the way they live. Paul not only wanted people to get saved, but he also concerned himself with their growth in faith. Act's 15:36

mentions how Paul wanted to go back and see how the converts were doing spiritually. Likewise, there are times when a teammate will disciple another player who desires to grow in his or her relationship with God. Such an occasion could arise because something has surfaced that needs immediate attention.

When it comes to teammates discipling teammates, it is always good to talk with the person who oversees the spiritual welfare of the team, to use and secure the appropriate tools for discipleship. Checking with the person in charge also allows the discipleship process to be guided in such a way that compliments the overall direction of ministry with the student-athletes. The director of spiritual development, character coach, chaplain and life skills coach will have a better grasp of how the athlete-to-athlete discipleship ministry should be conducted. What a joy for teammates to help other teammates grow in their faith.

How to Deal with Conflict:

At times when conflicts arise, when they surface it is important to respond to them properly. Conflicts come in various forms and at different times, even when you don't expect them. For this reason, we need a right perspective. The two ways to view conflict are from, a biblical perspective or a human perspective. When we see, hear, and experience opposition it provides us an opportunity to ask, what can I learn about God, myself, and others through the conflict?

Conflict can be a life-changing experience for everyone involved. While some troubles are self-inflicted, and others are not. In either case, it is essential to respond to them God's way. To depend on Him for the wisdom and insight to lead us through the conflict. The other option is to handle it on our own with a limited perspective. But the best way is to respond not react to it. This way God can use our struggles to help us grow in all relationships in life.

How to Build a Structure of Leadership:

When it comes to creating a process for developing leaders we must begin with the model Jesus established in the gospels. Jesus did not start with the masses to build leaders, he started by selecting a few individuals after spending all night in prayer. So, the first thing we must do as we begin to develop a structure for leadership is bathe the process in prayer. What prayer does, is helps us get God's direction as we begin developing leaders that we will help us do the work of the ministry.

Jeff Janssen says the following, *"The quality of your team's leadership dictates the rest of your athlete's work ethic, attitude, focus, confidence, mental toughness, team chemistry, and virtually all other aspects of your program."* 6

In establishing a structure for leadership, it is important to know what the plan will be for it to become a reality. The structure presented in this book includes a plan, purpose and process for developing leaders. First, the present leadership prays for potential leaders. Next, communication with present leaders moves the process along to observation. Observation begins when several players watch the way that candidate demonstrates leadership potential through everyday interaction with teammates and others. Usually, if someone is recommended by another leader on the team for a leadership position there is a good chance the observation will confirm the recommendation.

After communication and observation are complete, then dialogue with the potential leader is initiated by the person responsible for leadership development and recruitment on the athletic team. During this final stage the expectations, purpose and process are shared with the potential leader. A decision will follow shortly after that process is completed. Developing a team of leaders is about the most important activity any organization or team can do. It insures the legacy of God's desire to work through those He raised up to impact others on the team continues.

How to Develop Character in all Areas of Whole Person Development:

It doesn't make a difference who you are or where you are in the journey of life character is always important. You could be at work, home, church, or at the grocery store shopping, character is always essential. The same is true for the student-athlete, character is essential to display in all areas of Whole-Person Development.

Dallas Willard states, *"Character is that internal, overall structure of our self that reveals our long-running patterns of behavior"* 7

There will be times when your mind and body may not want to do what you are supposed to do at that moment, but your character will over ride those thoughts in those areas of your life. The following question is asked by student-athletes occasionally, is it wrong for your body or mind to not want to do something you have been asked to do? My answer would be no. Sometimes your body is telling something is wrong and it is good to listen to what it is saying. There are times when your physical condition will affect your spiritual condition. If you have just injured yourself there is a built-in defense mechanism that God has installed in you, that alerts you something is wrong with you physically. An athlete must know the difference between being hurt and sore. If your mind and body are telling you not to do something when you are hurt, character must be the driving force to help you do what you know and need to do. Character is vital to display in all areas of Whole Person Development.

Bill Hybel's writes, *"Character cannot be developed through good resolutions and checklists. It usually requires a lot of hard work, a little pain and years of faithfulness before any of the virtues are consistently noticeable in us."* 8

There may be a times when a student-athlete may not write a paper that is due in two days, may entertain the thought of not being honest about a certain situation, it even could be not wanting to read the bible or sleep in on a given Sunday morning. Do these thoughts mean something is wrong? It means character must be displayed in each of the scenarios presented. Character is the key component that drives each area of the Whole-Person Development model talked about throughout the book. Reputation may get someone to the top, but it is character that will keep one at the top. It doesn't matter if you are in a friendship, dating, engaged or married, it is character that allows one to deposit seeds of trust that will allow the relationships to grow. Keep developing character.!!!!

What Areas Should Student-Athletes Be Discipled?

> *How to Incorporate Spiritual Disciplines in Everyday Life*
> *How to Overcome Temptation*
> *How to Manage Time*
> *How to Live a Life of Servant Leadership*
> *How to Build Healthy Relationships*
> *How to Develop Spiritual and Natural Leadership*
> *How to Share a Personal Testimony and Present the Gospel*
> *How to Understand My Identity in Christ*
> *How to Disciple Another Teammate*
> *How to Deal with Conflict*
> *How to Build a Structure of Leadership*
> *How to Develop Character in All Areas Of Whole-Person Development*

Some Things to Ponder:

> *What Was One Thing I Learned from Reading the Chapter?*
> *How Will I Apply the One Thing I Have Learned from Reading the Chapter?*

Chapter Six

Who Should Disciple Student-Athletes?

Do you ever wonder if you are qualified to help a student-athlete? We all have a story to tell. Don't let your past keep you from sharing your story with others.

Coaches

Coaches often become a father figure for athletes today. There are times when the people who should have been role models in the lives of athletes are absent. God, in His providence, will then bring a coach to fill that role for an extended time.

John Ortburg says, *"There is a unique power in a conversation that happens face-to-face, one-on-one-one in private moments between two human beings."* [1]

The relationship the coach has with the player, allows him to have a great platform to speak truth in all areas of the athlete's life.

Athletic Staff Members

Sometimes the student-athlete feels more comfortable speaking with someone other than a coach. One thing a staff member must be careful of is not to undermine or undercut a decision a coach may have made regarding the player. We must show loyalty to the program in attitude and actions. We must learn to listen well, so we can provide good advice to the athlete in times of need. There are times we can help an athlete better understand what may be involved in the decision-making process as it relates to them and their coach. Many times, we help the athlete learn valuable lessons through conversations about life. There are other times when we can let the athletes know that God may use their experiences to teach them something about Himself, themselves and others. The conversation could often be non-related to the sport. Indeed, it becomes a teachable moment for everyone involved in the situation.

Former Players

It has been my experience when talking with an athlete about something he may be going through to inquire about the possibility of putting him in touch with a former player who may help the him better understand his situation. Sometimes a former player has been through a similar experience and can offer guidance during a tough moment or time in the players life. Other times an attempt to make contact is not due to a problem, but rather to get some insight from someone who can identify with a student-athlete. There are times it might be for an internship or job lead for an athlete. Other times it may just be to get a better perspective on life. At times a player will listen more to a former player rather than to someone involved in the present program. The former player brings a twofold perspective to the conversation; life in the sport as a former player and life after the sport as an alumnus. That conversation can be helpful to the athlete in the short and long term.

Chaplains / Character Coaches / and Life Skills Coaches

One thing that has always amazed me is who (people) and what (circumstances) God uses to bring about change in the lives of student-athletes. The question I find myself asking daily as I interact with athletes is who does God want to use to help this athlete figure out what he or she is going through? Sometimes it may be a teacher, coach, parent, character coach, teammate and other times it could be that spiritual leader who is serving with the team. It is a team effort and as each of us fulfill the role we have been given, God uses us to impact student-athletes in all areas of whole-person development.

Jim Stump says, *"You change the world by reshaping hearts and lives from the inside out. By walking with people on a daily basis, teaching them how to live by modeling a Christlike life."* 2

Teammates

There are times when athletes expect the coach or adult in their lives to say certain things. For example, as a chaplain, they expect me to talk to them about spiritual matters. However, I understand that, sometimes it is good for a student-athlete to hear from a fellow teammate, especially if the teammate has gone through circumstances they may be experiencing. The question we all need to ask as we minister to athletes is, "Who and what is God trying to use to bring about a change in the athlete life?"

Teachers / School Personnel and / Student Affairs Staff

Another person God may want to use in the life of a student-athlete is a teacher. Let us assume there has been an incident related to the classroom. The teacher has several options. First, the teacher could deal with the situation between the student and them self. Sometimes that is exactly what happens. Second, the teacher could involve a coach or any other adult to assist with the situation. Third, there are times when God will use a faculty member or someone in Student Affairs to be a part of the athlete's life-changing processes. As stated before, the fifty-dollar question that we all need to ask with regularity when dealing with players is, who (people) and what (circumstances) does God want to use to bring about a change in the athletes' life? There are other times when God will use someone outside the athletic program to make a difference in the life of a student-athlete. It is very important to pay attention to the who and what God may want to use to help a student-athlete grow through life experiences.

Who Should Disciple Student-Athletes?

➤ *Coaches*
➤ *Athletic Staff Members*
➤ *Former Players*
➤ *Chaplains / Character Coaches and / Life Skills Coaches*
➤ *Teammates*
➤ *Teachers / School Personnel, and/ Student Affairs Staff*

Some Things to Ponder:

➤ *What Was One Thing I Learned from Reading the Chapter?*
➤ *How Will I Apply the One Thing I Have Learned from Reading the Chapter?*

Chapter Seven

Things to Remember When Discipling Students-Athletes

The following insights will help you understand and develop a strategy for ministering to student-athletes in a very practical and simplified manner.

The Whole Team is Impacted Through Position Groups

The question often is asked," How do we influence the entire team?" After all, it is our desire to see the whole team impacted in all areas of whole-person development. In looking at the life and ministry of Jesus, we see a model He used to impact the world. He did not go to the masses to impact a few, but rather he selected a few and through them began to impact the masses. As we look at ways to impact our entire team, I think it is good that we look at the model Jesus used in His ministry. The application from Jesus' ministry that we apply to athletics is to influence the whole team through position groups. Regardless of the sport, it is my understanding that each team has specific groupings that make up the whole team. On some teams you may combine position groups because of the size of the individual groups. The one thing I like about this model is that it breaks the team up into smaller groupings. It not only breaks the team up into groups, but it also provides a workable and logistical process for impacting the whole team.

Tim Tebow writes, *"I have learned that, though God is in control of the big picture, I am responsible for how I use my platform, whatever its size – at the moment in time – to influence others" x* 1

This model is also used by Paul when writing to the Corinthian believers about how the body functions. It is about every individual person fulfilling the role that has been given to impact the whole body. Paul raises some great questions in the passage found in I Corinthians 12:12-27 that you can look at another time. Utilizing this model for discipling student-athletes will help us to focus more on the makeup of the individual groups and those who are in the position groups. The takeaway from the model Jesus and Paul used is that the greatest way to impact the whole team is through position groups.

Seek to Appoint a Spiritual Leader for Each Position Group

Once we understand how we impact the whole team, we can begin to give attention to the player who will be the spiritual leader in that position group. You may ask, "How do I select a spiritual leader for a position group?" There are several ways you can discover and select potential group leaders. The following three phases are what I use in recruiting spiritual leaders for each position group. It includes gathering information, effective communication, and observation that helps me to select the individual players to be position group leaders. This method can also be used in selecting spiritual minded athletes as well. It is a process that has proven to be invaluable for me as I continue to disciple young men on our football team. Let us jump into the how to's process of doing what I have just shared with you.

First, collect *information*, if possible, utilize a spiritual assessment questionnaire. This assessment could have six or seven questions on it from the general to specifics in nature. For example:

Do you have an idea of what you want to do after graduation?

- o No idea
- o Some idea
- o Have a good idea

Do you have a desire to meet for weekly discipleship?

- o No desire at this time
- o A little desire
- o A very high desire

Do you read your Bible?

- o Sometimes
- o Not at all
- o Regularly

These questions help you to assess where your student-athletes are at in their spiritual journey. It is not scientific, but it at least provides a starting point to identify potential spiritually-minded athletes in each position group.

Second, initiate *communication* with the present spiritual leader of the position group. During the discussion ask if he/she has seen anybody in the position group who might be a potential position group leader. The player may also be someone who in the future the baton might be handed to after the spiritual leader of that position group graduates. Do you notice you are starting a pipe line for developing group leaders? Sometimes, the position group leader will see spiritual leadership qualities in someone in the group that you may not have noticed. Once the person is discovered you can continue to have candid dialogue with the potential spiritual leader, eventually, set up a meeting with the individual player about the possibility of becoming the spiritual leader of the group. Which moves you right into the third step of the process.

Third, continue in *observation* after the player has been recommended, continue to observe the athlete in different situations. It has been my experience that when a position group leader suggests someone, there is good evidence to believe that your observation of the player is going to be a positive experience. Once the information, communication and observation process has been followed, you are then ready to move forward to engage in a conversation with the player who may eventually be a spiritual leader in that position group.

Meet Weekly with Spiritual Position Group Leaders for Discipleship

One of the requirements for the leader of a position group is to meet weekly with the Chaplain or character coach, etc. for at least 30 minutes. While engaged in the meeting there will be a time to talk about how things are going spiritually in the position group. It is also a time for prayer, discipleship, accountability, and encouragement. During the meeting, I ask myself several questions.

>What is God trying to do in the student-athlete's life? How is the athlete cooperating with what God is

trying to do in their life?

How can I be an encouragement to the athlete?

What I like about the meeting is that it provides an opportunity to teach something in a formal way, yet on the other hand, it also allows the freedom to have an open dialogue about the lesson or about life in general. There are times when a lesson is selected but we never get to the lesson because the Holy Spirit has another plan for that meeting. If that happens, we sometimes will do the lesson the following week or skip it and move on to what was supposed to be the plan for the following meeting. It is really a Life-on-Life time together, where one life influences another.

Teach the Position Group Spiritual Leader How to Be the Eyes and Ears in Their Position Group

As you disciple your spiritual leaders to do the work of the ministry with you, they become your eyes and ears in the position groups. As you talk about ministry together, your discussion becomes richer and deeper. They in one sense become an extension of your ministry. There are conversations you have with them that you may not have with other players in the position group. It is important for the spiritual leaders in the position group to know you respect and trust them. They need to know their opinions are important. It has been a real joy to see an athlete who was a spiritual leader of a position group become the spiritual leader of our entire football team. It is possible for a spiritual leader of a position group to also be a spiritual leader of the entire team. I have also had spiritual leaders who led it together. One leader would represent the offense and the other from the defensive side of the ball. But the leader of the athletic team may not always be someone presently a spiritual leader in a position group.

When selecting a spiritual leader for a position group or a leader for the athletic team, I always try to get an upperclassman or someone on scholarship and playing in the sport. The reason for doing this is that sometimes walk-on's or non-scholarship athletes are often intimidated by the scholarship players and starters. If for some reason, you are unable to select a player who meets that criteria you select the next best candidate, regardless of their status on the team. The key is to have players on scholarship or starters who lead by example and demonstrate servant leadership beginning in their position group. They can also continue to impact others through their position group and eventually the whole team.

One responsibility of the spiritual leader in the position group is to identify teammates in the High Interest group. Once identified, it is the leader's responsibility to pray with and for those in that group. It is also important for them to pray for those in the other two groups (Some interest and No interest) that God would give them favor through servant leadership, to encourage athletes to move up and out of those groups.

Encourage Spiritual Leaders to Make the Position Group Their Primary Ministry

In reflecting back on what has already been mentioned about impacting the whole team though position groups, it is very important to remind and encourage the leaders of position groups and other spiritually minded players in the position group to make their position group their primary ministry.

What this does for the athletes, it helps them to see their area of responsibility and ministry in a more realistic way. It takes some of the probability of being overwhelmed with numbers and provides a more practical way for them to minister to their teammates. The idea is to have players in each position group sowing seeds through servant leadership and prayer, therefore, trusting God to water the seeds that are being sown by faith and trusting Him to bring about fruit in His timing. What a motivation for giving God praise by seeing Him work through position groups to impact the whole team. That's what I call T.E.A.M: Together Everybody Achieves More.

Solicit Feedback from Spiritual Leaders on Position Group' Spiritual Welfare

One awesome benefit about developing relationships with your spiritual leaders is that they provide great insight about what is happening on ground level where the players live every day. They become a sounding board for you as you navigate through the ups and downs of ministry. Your leaders can also help you view situations from another perspective. I remember many times asking my spiritual leaders' questions that not only related to the position groups, but to the team as a whole and their insight was so helpful. In the process their feedback provides a window for them to see what the work of the ministry is all about.

Andy Stanley says, *"Self-evaluation is helpful, but evaluation from someone else is essential."* 2

Sometimes, there are discipline issues within the group that need to be addressed. Other times, there are leadership changes that need to take place in the group. As you continue to build healthy relationships with your spiritual leaders, you help them prepare for future ministry after graduation. What a joy to model the kind of leadership they can look back on and say, I saw it done the right way. This is where your ministry to the student-athlete brings forth fruit later in life.

Inspire Spiritually-Minded Athletes in Position Groups to Support Their Leaders

It is critical for those who are spiritually minded to support the spiritual leader of their position group. Support for their leader can include encouragement and servant leadership. Spiritually minded athletes help lead by example, thus opening doors for them to compliment what God is doing in and through the life of the spiritual leader and spiritually minded players in their position group. They begin by leading themselves, then they continue asking God for opportunities to serve their position group to have His favor with those athletes. It is all about them working together to bring about the most impact through their position groups. As the saying goes: "Team work makes the dream work. "

Earn the Right to Speak into Lives of Student-Athletes

There are some who think just because they have a position it automatically gives them the right to be heard by student-athletes. Well, that is not the case in real life. The truth of the matter is that a person's position provides an opportunity to speak truth into the lives of others, but they must learn how to earn the right to speak into the lives of athletes through who they are as a person. An appointed leader earns the right to speak truth into the lives of others through servant leadership.

James Kouzes writes, *"The most important personal quality people look for and admire in a leader is credibility If people don't believe in the messenger, they won't believe in the message."* 3

I remember serving as a police chaplain for 11 years in my hometown, New Bedford, Mass. My father was a former cop in the same Police Department for 29 years before retiring. I had to look for creative ways to build relationships and trust with the police officers if I was to have a fruitful ministry while serving as their chaplain. Over time, God gave me wonderful favor in the officers' eyes because I built meaningful relationships through consistent dialogue while visiting officers on all three shifts at the station. It also meant showing up at different police related events during the year, visiting someone in the hospital, or attending the funeral of a member of the police officer's family. Those are the kind of acts of kindness that allow someone to speak into the life of another. Your position may be the platform that opens the door to speak, but who you are as a person is the best way to earning the right to speak into the lives of your players. Do not just talk about it, let your life experiences be about it every day while serving Him and others.

Keep the Conversations Confidential Unless Given Permission to Share

Confidentiality is very important when having conversations with student-athletes. As a rule, when having a conversation with student athletes, I attempt to keep the conversation confidential unless it is something that the head coach needs to know. The last thing you want is for you to know something and the head coach get blindsided. If there is something that could affect the team in a negative way, then you must ask God for wisdom to either ask the student athlete to speak with the head coach or offer to go with the athlete to speak with the head coach about the matter. Furthermore, if there is an issue, I attempt to deal with it and if I cannot solve it, I go up the chain. I will first start with the position coach, if not successful then the next person will be the coordinator and if need be, the head coach. It is always good to follow that protocol when dealing with a situation that could be both negative and positive. It helps to maintain integrity within your athletic team.

Look for Imaginative Ways to Encourage and Add Value to Student-Athletes

In ministry sometimes, it is easy to focus on the negative that take place on the team. We cannot allow ourselves to fall into that trap, we must think right so we do not get tricked by the enemy. More so, we need to make a habit of finding athletes doing right things and use those positive examples to encourage them as they live out the mission and vison of the athletic program. Who does not need encouragement?

Another important ingredient to exhibit in ministry is adding value to others through Christ-like attitudes and actions. Every athlete has the potential to add value to the team. When thinking about adding value, I refer to the athlete living out the four components of whole-person development in front of teammates. Some athletes add more value in areas of whole person development than others. But as we use the whole-person development model, we can assess what kind of value is being added or not being added to the team as a whole.

As a reminder, the four components of whole-person development are academic, athletic, social and spiritual. Those are the principal areas of a student-athlete's life while participating in the sport. Looking at the athlete's life through those lenses will help us to keep the main thing the main thing.

Never Underestimate the Time It Takes to Develop Spiritual Leaders

When we consider the process of developing spiritual leaders, it is important to remember it takes a lot of time, effort, prayer and faithfulness. Reflecting on the time it takes for a baby to go from infancy to adulthood is staggering as we ponder all that went into the maturation process. It takes the same time, if not more, to grow spiritual leaders on our team. It takes more time than meets the eye. I remember starting a project at home, and when I finally completed the task, I had no idea how much had passed in finishing the job.

Rod Dempsey shares, *"The ultimate success for a small group leader is to simultaneously grow your group in quality and quantity while developing future leaders."* 4

Considering all that goes into developing leaders, we need to be reminded that the time is worth it. We get a chance to invest in, not only while they are a part of our program, but for their future ministry. What a great motivation for investing in the discipleship of athletes.

71

Talk with Spiritual Leaders about Successors of Their Position Group

When replacing a spiritual leader of a position group, it is talked and prayed about long before the decision must be made. One responsibility of the group's spiritual leader and of the decision maker is to be in constant dialogue about the matter. Multiplication and reproduction of spiritual leaders is a top priority in perpetuating the spiritual leadership on any athletic team. Hopefully, the replacement will be someone groomed to assume that spiritual leadership position from within the position group.

Once someone in the group has been identified as a possible replacement, the present spiritual leader in the group begins to talk with and spend time with the potential leader. Soon afterward the Chaplain or person responsible for the spiritual oversight of the team will also begin to talk with the potential spiritual leader. Usually, when someone is recommended from within the group, there seems to be a consensus among the spiritual leaders. When the athlete has been selected, the one-on-one meetings continue to take place with the spiritual overseer of the team. Working together helps the spiritual leadership in the position groups continue to be strong as one seeks to make a spiritual difference in the lives of student-athletes by developing spiritual leaders on the team.

Things to Remember When Discipling Student-Athletes

> ➤ *The Whole Team is Impacted Through Position Groups*
> ➤ *Seek to Appoint a Spiritual Leader for Each Position Group*

- *Meet Weekly with Spiritual Position Group Leaders for Discipleship*
- *Teach the Position Group Spiritual Leader how to be Eyes and Ears in Their Position Group*
- *Encourage Spiritual Leaders to Make Position Groups Their Primary Ministry*
- *Solicit Feedback from Spiritual Leaders on the Position Groups' Spiritual Welfare*
- *Inspire Spiritual-Minded Athletes in Position Group to Support Their Spiritual Leaders*
- *Earn the Right to Speak into Lives of Student-Athletes*
- *Keep the Conversations Confidential Unless Given Permission to Share*
- *Look for Imaginative Ways to Encourage and Add Value to Student-Athlete*
- *Never Underestimate the Time it Takes to Develop Spiritual Leaders*
- *Talk with Spiritual Leaders about Successors of Their Position Group*

Some Things to Ponder:

- *What Was One Thing I Learned from Reading the Chapter?*
- *How Will I Apply the One Thing I Have Learned from Reading the Chapter?*

Chapter Eight

The Nuts and Bolts for Effective Discipleship Ministry to Student-Athletes

In this chapter, you will find foundational principles for having an effective ministry with student-athletes. They will guide you as you serve Him and others.

Seek to Understand and Implement the Whole Person Development Model

The whole-person development approach is both biblical and foundational when it comes to discipling student-athletes. It is biblical because it is based on Luke 2:52. In the verse, there are four areas that are to be emphasized: *Wisdom, Stature, God and Man. Wisdom* will refer to the athlete's mind (Academic Life). *Stature* will refer to the student-athlete's physical life (Athletic Life). *God* will refer to the athlete's spiritual life (Spiritual Life), and *Man* will refer to the student-athlete's social life (Social Life).

Ed Gomes, *"Seeking to understand the Whole-Person Development model sets one up for a balanced and biblical ministry to athletes and allows one to stay on task as we meet the needs in all four areas of the student athlete."* 1

The goal is for God to use the following areas to develop Christlikeness or character in the life of the player. Each one of the four areas have a component or outcome that is precise. The *academic* component is to help the student-athlete acquire an education for life after competing in the sport. The *athletic* component is to help the student-athlete prepare physically and mentally to compete in the athletic event. The *spiritual* component is to help the student-athlete foster growth through spiritual and biblical character development. The *social* component is to help the student-athlete appropriate positive interaction with fellow students, faculty and community.

While thinking and praying about a way to illustrate the whole-person development model, God gave me an illustration that fits the model well. The illustration has to do with the four tires on an automobile. The key to experiencing the best ride in your vehicle is to have the right amount of air pressure in each tire. To not have the right amount of air pressure in each tire is to experience a bumpy ride. Some of the negative aspects of not having the right amount of pressure in the tires could be that the car could swerve to one side of the road, the wear on the tires could become uneven, and lack of good gas mileage, to only name a few. On the other hand, to have the proper amount of air pressure in the tires would result in the very opposite type of ride. Tires that are properly inflated will produce a more balanced ride.

The aspiration of each student-athlete should be to add value to the team through each of the four areas of whole-person development. Some players may not start out adding value in all four areas, however, it should be the desire of those working with the student-athlete to see that happen. Sometimes athletes are only adding value in a few of those areas. The area that you don't see the athlete adding value is the area you need to ask God for wisdom to help the player move in that direction. Just about everything a player is involved in throughout his or her athletic career is connected to one of the four areas of whole-person development.

A few of the central questions I find myself asking all the time as I minister to players are, what is God trying to do in these four areas of the athlete's life? How is the student-athlete cooperating with what God is trying to do in all four major areas of his or her life? How does God want to use me to help the player live out the whole-person development components in front of others?

The whole-person development approach allows each of us to focus on the four primary areas of the players life. It keeps us from getting bogged down with a lot of things that could side track us from focusing on the main thing while ministering to the student-athlete in a positive manner.

Utilize the Whole Person Development Questions for Coaches, Leaders and Players

The questions for the players and those working with student-athletes provide a great opportunity for dialogue in all areas of whole-person development. The questions are designed to initiate interaction with student-athletes about life and give the player something to think about as well. The whole-person development assessment tool is another instrument that can be used by the athlete, coach or leader working with the athlete for honest evaluation in all four areas of the athlete's life.

Be Cognizant of the Three Groupings of Student-Athletes on Each Team

One of the greatest ways to begin to effectively disciple athletes, is being able to utilize a practical and systematic method for identifying what group the athlete may be in on the team. This approach is not scientific, but it provides the capability to have a starting point to meet the spiritual, social, academic and athletic needs of the student-athlete. The names of the three groups are *High Interest, Some Interest and No Interest.* The High Interest group of players are intentional about their relationship with God and want to make an impact on the team. The *Some Interest* group of players are not intentional about developing their relationship with God, however would indicate experienced salvation. The *No Interest* group of players have never been born again.

You may be asking how the players are placed in a group after they have been identified. The three groups of student-athletes are identified by a three-way process which includes information, communication and observation. As mentioned earlier, information is gathered through a spiritual assessment questionnaire, communication takes place with the position group spiritual leaders, and observation takes place through everyday interactions with players. Once this process has been followed, the Chaplain, Character coach or Life skills coach can begin to have follow up conversations with those athletes.

The athletes who are identified in the high interest group are asked if they are willing to meet for 30 minutes once a week for discipleship. During the 30-minute discipleship meeting, you go from the general to the specifics. The general would include questions about the week, family and any other topics that may come up at the beginning of the discipleship meeting. The weekly discipleship meeting may consist of one to four players in the group. The person who picks the discipleship lesson from the *Building A Legacy* manual gets to ask anyone in the group a question about life. The question doesn't have to do with the lesson, but sometimes it may be related to the lesson. One of the questions could be as general as, who have you encouraged in a verbal or nonverbal way this week? Another more specific question could be, in the last seven days have you looked at anything on the computer that you should not be looking at? Once the question has been asked, we proceed with the lesson for the day. At the end of the lesson, a prayer is offered by someone in the group. There are times when a lesson is not completed because of something may have come up during the discussion time. If that is the case, you can continue the lesson the next time you meet, or just move to what was planned for the next week's meeting. It's not about getting through the lesson, it is about listening to the Holy Spirit during the discipleship time together. After a lesson is selected and completed, the following week we have a time of open dialogue. During that meeting, all we do is talk about life. There is no agenda other than sharing life together. The opportunity to share life together has proven very helpful in developing relationships with student athletes. Confidentiality is asked of each player in discipleship meetings. The group setting is really Life-on-Life.

It is important to continue to earn the right to speak into the lives of the athletes who are in the Some and No interest groups through servant leadership and constant dialogue. The dialogue could take place while in the locker room, during practice or while having something to eat. Although you may be primarily meeting with players for weekly discipleship who are in the high interest group, you are always looking to see other players move into the High interest group.

Remember to Use the Spiritual Assessment Tool for Players

The spiritual assessment tool can be used by the individual player and coach. The tool provides an opportunity for the player and coach to assess where the player is in all areas of whole-person development. Once the assessment has been administered, there is a great time of dialogue between the coach and the player about the assessment. It is possible that the player could be adding value in one or more areas of the model, and the assessment could also reveal an area that needs attention in the life of the student. It is a very practical tool that helps coaches and players look honestly into all for areas of whole-person development.

Be Aware of Whole Person Development Components

The whole-person development components (Academic, Athletic, Social, and Spiritual) represent the four major areas of a student-athletes athletic experience. Just about everything said and done within the sport is related to one of the four areas. When I talk with our athletes I try to pay attention to what is going on in each of those areas mentioned. The key is for each player to add value to the team by reflecting positive attitudes and actions in each of the whole-person development areas.

Is it possible for a player to give more attention to one area more than the others? Absolutely, however the objective is to be balanced in all four areas. There are times when things will come up which reflect negative and positive behavior. The behaviors will be addressed accordingly by someone within the program. To be intentional in the following areas with purpose will allow the student-athlete to have a life changing experience.

Be Mindful How God Uses People and Situations to Shape Student-Athletes

One of the greatest joys anyone can have in serving God and others is the opportunity to make a spiritual impact in the life of student-athletes. To be used by God to make a difference in the life of an athlete cannot be compared to anything else in life. To see athletes born again and then grow in their faith is awesome, to say the least. Going from no spiritual life to possessing spiritual life is miraculous. In short, it is divine!!!! As we serve students and coaches, it's important to remember that God wants to use us to influence others for the kingdom. It is also important for coaches and leaders to be reminded that sometimes God wants to use the players to bring about change in our lives of coaches and leaders. We as parents sometime thought it was just us teaching our children about life, but there were times when God was using our children to teach us a thing or two about life as well. It goes both ways. God uses all kinds of people and circumstances to develop Christlikeness and character in the lives of those we serve. The key is to pay attention to whom and what He desires to use to bring about change.

Barry Black states, *"Many want a testimony without a test, but testimonies are usually forged in the furnace of afflicted."* 2

God desires to use a person or situation to bring about salvation in the life of others. Other times he may use a person or situation to help an athlete become more Christlike or develop a character quality in the life of the player you are dealing with. I am reminded of Joseph in the prison cell with the baker and the butler. Joseph was available to help two people interpret what they were going through in life, they had no clue. The same is true for the person who is available to be used by God. That is exactly what God does; He uses the person to help others interpret life according to His will and plan.

Live Out Your Biblical Philosophy and Mindset for Discipling Student-Athletes

When developing a philosophy of ministry or a proper mindset for ministry, there must be a clear and consistent understanding of a biblical point of view in the mind and heart of those serving God and others. Being sure about this will help to weather the storms of life while in ministry. Some of those storms could be reflective in living a life of faith or living a life of doubt, focusing on what isn't happening in the lives of athletes, or focusing on what could happen in the lives of our student athletes, not seeing the results that you want to see, personal failures, and disappointments of some form, to name a few possible storms in ministry. A great example of having the right approach to ministry is Joseph while in the prison with the Butler and the Baker. There are valuable lessons we can learn from Joseph that help us be confident and secure in what we are doing to minster to student athletes found in Genesis 39:4-23. First, from a human point of view, Joseph should not have been in prison. However, God had another plan for him and he did not let his human circumstances keep him from being used by God to impact others. The same is true for those who are involved in the work of the ministry.

The Butler and the Baker had an experience that aroused their curiosity, and Joseph was there to help them interpret what was happening in their lives. The same is true for anyone who makes himself or herself available for God's work. God allows people to intersect in our lives and because of that human contact, God uses us to make a difference. God places athletes on teams to impact other players for His glory. Having that philosophy and mindset of God enables Him to use us in the lives of others. That's why I can better understand why Jesus calls us to be light and salt today. We should bloom where we have been planted that we may take the light that He has given us and pass it on to others. We are to be Salt and Light by the way we live, to earn the right to speak into the lives of those we minister to daily.

Believe God Desires to Use You to Impact Student-Athletes

It is very important to remember that God desires for you to impact student-athletes. This belief is foundational for being used by God and to have the kind of favor with God and athletes you desire. Think about what the opposite kind of thinking could be as you minister to athletes. This is not positive thinking, it is biblical thinking for the person who wants to be used by God to make a difference. It is having

82

the right kind of motivation; a heart attitude that focuses on the Father's business. Some have called this thinking, doing the work of the ministry from a faith base and not a doubt base. We either operate out of faith or we are operating out of doubt. Faith believes that God has called us, and we are trusting Him for His results. Doubt assumes the very opposite and that is the enemy's system of thinking.

In other words, we are trusting God to do in the lives of student-athletes only what He can do. What a joy to be a part of what God is doing through and in us as we serve Him and players. Some have also called those kind of interactions divine appointments. I am all for those kinds of appointments in life. We see this in the life of Jesus as a twelve-year-old boy while sitting in the temple, listening and asking questions while his parents were looking for him. After his parents had located and had some dialogue with Him about what they had been though prior to finding Him, He responded with a very profound statement in Luke 2:41-50. We also see this belief illustrated in the life of Joseph when he was in prison with the Butler and the Baker in Genesis 40:1-23. There are times when things may not be going the way you want them to in the life of a student-athlete, but you must be faithful where you have been planted and trust God for His results.

Remember to Incorporate Character Qualities into the Whole Person Development Model

One of the unwavering qualities in all four areas of whole-person development is the character piece. Character impacts all four of the areas of the model. Character affects the totality of life beyond the sport. To add the kind of value that defines a program and its culture has a lot to do with the individual characters of the participants. Everybody's character can have a negative or positive effect on the program. The greater the character, the greater the probabilities for the team to reflect Christlikeness and character through the wins and losses.

Mel Lawrenze writes, *"Character traits are built over a long period of time by sustained repetition of right instincts and the matching sets. Character is built by progressive patterning of a person's life."* 3

It is important to utilize the character qualities in dealing with student-athletes. The character you seek to develop in the student-athletes will last a life time. They may not understand what you are attempting to do then, but later in life they will better understand what you were trying to instill in them through whatever sport they participated in.

The Nut's and Bolt's Effective Discipleship Ministry to Student-Athletes

- ➢ *Seek to Understand and Implement the Whole Person Development Model*
- ➢ *Utilize the Whole Person Development Questions for Coaches, Leaders and Players*
- ➢ *Be Cognizant of the Three Groupings of Student-Athlete's on Each Team*
- ➢ *Remember to Use the Spiritual Assessment Tool for Players*
- ➢ *Be aware of Whole Person development Components*
- ➢ *Be Mindful How God Uses People and Situations to Shape Student-Athletes*

> ➤ *Live Out Your Biblical Philosophy and Mindset for Discipling Student-Athletes*
> ➤ *Believe God Desires to Use You to Impact Student-Athletes*
> ➤ *Remember to Incorporate Character Qualities into the Whole Person Development Model*

Some Things to Ponder:

> ➤ *What Was One Thing I Learned from Reading the Chapter?*
> ➤ *How Will I Apply the One Thing I Have Learned from Reading the Chapter?*

Chapter Nine

Questions to Consider When Discipling Student-Athletes

Have you ever doubted your ministry to student-athletes? Maybe the following questions and answers will eliminate any of your doubts as you move forward in your calling.

Which Student-Athletes Do I Start the Discipleship Ministry With?

Start with those who have a desire (High Interest) to grow in their relationship with Christ and interest in being used by God to make a difference on the team. As mentioned, there are several ways to identify those athletes who would be in the high interest group. Once you start with that group, you will have dialogue with other athletes and you will begin to involve them in your discipleship process as well. You can utilize the spiritual assessment questionnaire to help in this area also. Remember Jesus started with twelve and he impacted the world.

How Should I Respond When an Athlete Displays A Lack of Interest in Discipleship at Times?

In situations like this, you begin by asking God for wisdom. Sometimes, God will let us see, hear or experience something with purpose. Once you have prayed about what you are seeing or hearing, you may seek to engage in a conversation with the athlete. You can begin with a question that is positive in nature. The reason I say positive in nature is because anybody, especially a student- athlete, can become overwhelmed with the expectations in all areas of whole-person development. Once you have asked the question or questions, you can better understand what is going on in the athlete's life. During the conversation you may need to encourage or challenge the student-athlete to make the necessary adjustments to keep the discipling process going. You may have to adjust your meeting times to accommodate the athlete's schedule. The point is, you use what you see to encourage the player to learn valuable lessons from what has been brought up in the conversation. If the athlete chooses not to meet anymore, for whatever reason, you always keep the door open and continue to pray for him or her. You always keep the door open for something to change or for somebody else to step in and begin to pick up where you left off in making a spiritual impact in the athlete's life.

What Should I Do When I Don't Have a Spiritual Leader for a Position Group?

You continue to look in the position group for a potential spiritual leader for the group. It is very important to wait on God to bring that person to you. There are times when you could be meeting with a potential spiritual leader in the group, but the athlete is just not ready to assume that role. Another thing you can do is ask spiritual leaders of other position groups to pray with you about the need. In the meantime, you trust God to raise someone up to fulfill that role in His timing.

When Do I Involve the Coaches and Support Staff in the Discipleship Ministry?

As God provides the opportunity to share your ministry with the head coach, coaches, and support staff you can give them an overview of what you are doing and how you are doing it. Sometimes you may ask the head coach for an opportunity to present what you are doing to help players grow in their faith. There will be other times when you are having dialogue with coaches or support staff about what is going on in the spiritual life of a player and you will be able to involve them in the life transforming process of discipleship. A coach, at times, may ask an athlete to sit down with you for a period of time to walk through some issues they may be experiencing. There are many opportunities for athletic staff members to be involved in the discipleship process. Other times there may be people outside the athletic staff that may be a part of the discipleship process that is taking place with the teams as well. One of the key questions you always want to be asking during the discipleship process is, who are some other people God may want to use to bring about change in the lives of student-athletes? This is an important question because others can provide a different perspective in the lives of those you are discipling.

How Do I Deal with Discouragement in the Discipleship Ministry?

One of the most important things to remember when dealing with discouragement in ministry is thinking correctly about God, self, and others. The enemy will attempt to get whatever and whoever it is to get their focus out of balance. We may not be able to control all the thoughts that surface, but one thing we can do is properly interpret those thoughts. How we interpret those thoughts is by asking the right questions. If we ask the right questions about God, self, and others, there is a great chance we will get the right answer. If we ask the wrong questions about God, self, and others, there is good chance we will get the wrong answers.

Clay Scroggins says, *"A distorted identity will cause you to think too lowly or too highly of yourself, when the goal is to think rightly."* 1

The *first* thing in dealing with discouragement is to make sure we are asking the right questions. An example of asking the wrong question about God may be, why are You allowing me to think like this? It is okay to ask God questions? A correct question when going through times could be, God, what can I learn about You through this moment of discouragement? When I ask that question I begin to realize that He is loving, holy, all powerful, and sovereign, and I begin to use God given reason to understand that I could be going through this so that I can learn something about our heavenly Father. When I begin to think like that I can begin to respond to whatever it is the enemy is trying to use to discourage me. One of his tricks is to get us to ask the wrong questions, because he knows what that kind of reasoning could lead to in ministry.

The *second* thing that I would do in dealing with discouragement is to evaluate how I am thinking about myself. If I am not thinking correctly about who I am in Christ, I can begin to set myself up for discouragement. Understanding who I am is Christ is all about looking at the way God looks at each of us. He looks at us through Christ because at the moment of salvation we were transferred from the kingdom of darkness into the kingdom of light. We are no longer children of the devil, but rather, have become children of God. My identity is about who I am in Christ. Recognizing who I am in Christ provides hope to face and deal with whatever the enemy is trying to use to discourage me. You see, his game plan is for us to think incorrectly, and if he can get us to do that, he will. There have been times when we may have allowed people or circumstances to determine our value or who we are, we must remember that God and God alone determines who we are and our value.

Thirdly, I would look at how I am viewing those I am discipling. When I don't view athletes correctly, it affects the way I think about them. I must remember that God has allowed us to cross paths so that His will can be fulfilled in each of their lives. There are times when I don't see things happening like I would like to see them happening in the lives of our student-athletes. Those are times when I go to God in prayer and ask Him to help me see the athlete or situation from His perspective and He begins to help me understand that He is control. Remember, spiritual warfare is real in the work of the ministry. It was something Jesus and others, like the apostle Paul, dealt with. So, if that is something they dealt with, you can be assured that we will encounter those spiritual battles in the ministry that we have as well. During times of discouragement it is important to read the normal gauges of life correctly. Just as we all have gauges in our automobiles. If your gas gauge is reading low, you have a few options. One, is to go to a gas station and put gas in your tank. That is interpreting what the gauge is telling you about the amount of gas you have in your tank. Secondly, reach into the glove compartment and pull out the small hammer and knock the light or gauge out, so you don't see it anymore. Think about how you are going to read that gauge. We have two choices, we can do ministry living in the real world or we can do ministry living in a dream world. The real world is doing ministry like it really is, *(The ups and downs of ministry)* doing ministry in a dream world is doing the work of the ministry like I wished it was. It is possible for my spiritual gauge to be fine and my emotional gauge to be reading low? The key question is to honestly ask; what is the gauge trying to tell me? Some of the gauges we must read properly and regularly are the emotional, relational, family, financial, mental, ministry, physical, psychological, and spiritual gauges. Another thing you may want to do is seek a medical opinion because it could be something that needs a physician's attention. If you are not able to work through what you are going through, my advice would be to talk with a trusted friend or seek professional help from a spiritual counselor. Don't let the enemy keep you from fulfilling the role that God has placed you in as an ambassador for Him.

How Do I Make a Smooth Transition When Changing a Spiritual Leader in a Position Group?

This kind of situation doesn't happen a lot, but every so often after observing a player in the leadership role as the spiritual leader of a position group, you may have to make a change in leadership roles within the position group for one reason or another. The change is not always made because of some moral failure or lack of spiritual commitment to the group, but it may have to do with personality or lack of leadership skills. It may mean that someone else better fits the social and leadership qualifications of the spiritual group has risen up. This decision is not an easy decision to make, however, every so often it needs to be made. Here are some practical suggestions on how to make that kind of decision.

Bill Hybels shares, *"Leadership development never happens accidently. It only happens when some leader has a white-hot vision for it."* 2

The first and most important thing to do is bathe the decision in prayer. Once you have spent a good amount of time in prayer, you may want to talk with the position coach, another coach or a support staff member who you respect spiritually. It is assumed that you have sought out the counsel of at least one other person before speaking with the athlete about what is on your mind. The next thing I would do is set up a meeting with the spiritual leader you need to speak with. You want to share what has been on your mind and you want to also get his input on what you have been thinking about. It is very possible that after sharing your heart with the student-athlete, there may be an agreement about the decision you are thinking about making for the position group. Another possibility could be the athlete might agree to work on the areas that have given you concern. It is important to express from the beginning of the meeting what you appreciate about the athlete. The individual must know that you have a genuine love and concern for them. It's vital to express that this has not been an easy thing to talk about, but because of the relationship you have with each other, it's the right thing to do. I have had to make this move on one occasion and it went smoothly. I think it went smoothly because the athlete knew that I had a genuine interest in him as a person. The athlete that was moved into the position had the favor of the person and the rest of the spiritually minded athletes in the group. When everybody involved knows you want the best, it seems to help in making the transition a little easier.

What Should I Do if I Don't See the Results in My Discipleship Ministry?

One of the things that we must understand up front is that God expects us to be faithful where we have been planted. Yes, it is okay to desire success in our discipleship ministry with student athletes, however, we must remember that it is about being faithful with what and who we have been entrusted to serve. As we continue to sow seeds into the lives of those we are working with, God has a way of bringing the fruit to the surface. It is our responsibility to sow the seeds and let Him bring the harvest. (1 Cor. 3:5-10, 4:1-2) What an honor for us to cooperate with God as we serve the student-athletes we are working with every day. May each of us be found faithful in making disciples where we have been planted.

How Do I Help a Spiritual Leader Who Has Failed in One of the Areas of Whole Person Development?

First, ask God for wisdom to properly respond to what has taken place. Second, examine God's Word to get His perspective on what has happened. Third, continue to ask God for wisdom to communicate honestly and biblically with the person or persons involved in the situation. Fourth, provide a biblical and practical response to what has taken place. Fifthly, you set up accountability to help the person follow through with the biblical and practical instruction that was given. In short, you continue to trust the process God has given you to help the athlete get back on their feet, spiritually speaking.

Bob Reccord writes, *"God powers our inner being with an alarm system. It's set to sound a warning when we're in danger of crossing over the well-intentioned boundaries He has established for our lives."* 3

What Are Some Possible Outcomes from Discipling Student-Athletes?

When I talk about outcomes I am talking about those things that have been learned and observed by athletes during the discipleship process that can be transferable after competing in their sport. In other words, what the disciple has seen modeled that can be applied to life after the athlete has moved on to the next phase in the journey of life. Many times, lessons are easily caught than taught. What a constant reminder to each of us who are involved in discipling student-athletes these days. Each of us should live out what we are expecting our players to live out after they leave from being under our tutelage. It is always good to communicate to those we are discipling what the overall game plan is for them to be able to take what has been passed on through verbal and non-verbal communication and reproduced elsewhere. Some of the places where those things can be reproduced are in the individual life of the former athlete, present ministry, local church or place of employment. It is important to remind the student-athlete about the outcomes during the discipleship development.

Greg Ogdon writes, *"Maturity is the end product and that is what Paul is attempting to produce..."* 4

Sometimes there are things that you may be modeling or teaching the athlete that won't be understood until later in life. Those things may have come from a lesson you taught, a life experience, or just something that happened to be a teachable moment during the time engaged in the life-on-life relationship of discipleship.

How Do I Teach Spiritually-Minded Athletes to Support What God is Doing on the Athletic team?

In thinking about harnessing the support from spiritually minded teammates, it's important for the spiritual leaders of position groups to encourage their support. Not only is it the responsibility of the spiritual leaders, but also the obligation of the spiritually-minded teammates to become a part of what God is doing in and through them, first in their position group and then on the team. In a nut shell, it is key to remind them that they are part of a group of athletes binding together to see God use them to impact teammates on the team. It is called earning the right to be heard by sowing seeds through acts of kindness throughout their athletic experience. One act of kindness could be as simple as remembering the birthdays of teammates in the position group and on the team. Doing the little things are essential, so that the important things become a reality while serving Him and others on the team.

How Do I Appoint a Spiritual Leader for the Entire Team?

This is a very important question to ask because it impacts the team in all areas of whole- person development. There are times when more than one person is selected to be a spiritual leader of the team. It doesn't have to be two players, but that is an option. Here are some things to look for when trying to select someone to be the spiritual leader of your team. The first thing to look for is someone on the team who is respected in all areas of whole-person development. It is always good to have someone, if on a college level, who is on scholarship, contributing in the sport or an upper-class teammate. There are times when the person or persons may not meet the criteria. I think the bottom line would be someone who has earned the respect of teammates because their walk before God and teammates is consistent with the Word and expectations of the spiritual overseer of the team. In this process, you look for leadership skills that will complement the position to be assumed, however, there may be potential that you see that can be developed while fulfilling that role. Sometimes this person may be a spiritual leader of a position group and other times the person may not hold that position because of seniority in the position group, spiritually speaking. Remember, the most spiritually minded athlete is not always the most athletically gifted player on the team. Ask God and others for wisdom as you seek to fulfill that position on your team.

How Do I Practice the Ministry of Presence with Student-Athletes?

It is very important to understand as we minister to our student-athletes. To practice the presence of ministry, we must be aware of places and situations that our athletes find themselves in now. At times, it may be in the locker room just encouraging athletes. Other times, it may be during practice, in the library, or just walking with an athlete and having a normal conversation about life. There are moments when practicing the presence of ministry is important because an athlete has received some bad news from home, or it could be a personal injury to the athlete that might end his or her athletic career. Practicing the presence of ministry is very important during the loss of a loved one or when an athlete is going in for surgery. At times it means just being there and saying nothing other than maintaining an attitude of prayer and sensitivity to what the student-athlete is going through at that moment. It may mean that, after a while, you offer a prayer on behalf of what the athlete is experiencing at the time. One of the many ministry qualities we see in the life of Jesus is the ministry of presence; Jesus being at the right place at the right time to meet a need at that moment. There were times when Jesus did ministry with His disciples present as found in Luke 8:49-56. May we be like Jesus in this area of our ministry as we serve Him and others.

How Do I Deal with Moments of Doubt When Discipling Student-Athletes?

This is a very important question to think through when it comes to discipleship. If the enemy can get you to doubt what God has led you and I to do when it comes to discipling players, that's exactly where he wants us to be in our thinking. He is the master at attempting to get us to doubt what we believe to be God's will, discipling athletes. We see his tactic in the first book of the Bible, in the Garden of Eden. He sought to get Adam and Eve to doubt what God had said to them about following the instructions He had given them. His strategy is to try to get us to allow our mind and heart to focus on things that create doubt. It is an old trick that he continues to use today.

My wife's Dad would always say, *"The Devil doesn't have any new tricks, he is just good at the old tricks."* 5

If God has given you something to do, you can expect the enemy to use doubt to keep you from being about the Father's business in discipling student-athletes. We may not be able to control all the thoughts that come to mind, but we can interpret the thoughts that come to our mind. The way we interpret the thoughts is by asking the correct questions related to the doubt. Some of the possible questions could be as follows; where is the doubt coming from? What has precipitated the doubt in the first place? Is the doubt a result of me looking at what isn't happening instead of what is happening in the ministry of discipleship? Once these types of questions have been asked, then you begin to better understand where and why the doubts have surfaced. During that process, you may discover that the doubt is a lack of faith and trick of the enemy to keep you from being faithful and living by faith. I have learned that if God has given you clear direction, expect the enemy to try to use moments of doubt to keep you from fulfilling the vision God may have given you. There are times when we may not see something happening in the lives of those we are attempting to disciple, therefore, God may want you or I to have a very honest and open conversation with the athlete or someone else who may provide some biblical insight as to why there is doubt. Don't let the enemy try to use one of his old tricks to keep you from being faithful to what God has called you to do. Remember, it's about faithfulness and leaving the results in God's hands. Do your best and let God take care of the rest.

What Are Some Frustrations in Discipling Student-Athletes?

I wish I could always tell you that everything in discipling student-athletes goes the way we expect it to go. Let me ask you a question. Isn't that the way life is at times? You come out of the house on your way to a meeting and find you have a flat tire? Well, the reality of the matter is that in discipleship, things don't go the way we think they should go. However, we have a responsibility to look at life from God's perspective. Here are a few of the frustrations of discipling student-athletes; athletes whose talk doesn't match their walk, a lack of properly responding to failure, complacency regarding spiritual matters, displaying a know-it-all attitude through words and actions, not taking responsibility for negative behavior, and athletes who don't utilize the opportunity to develop their relationship with God as they should.

It is important during times of frustrations to maintain a good attitude towards those we are working with. To not have the right attitude only makes the situation worse. It is during these frustrations that we get a chance to evaluate what God is trying to do in the life of the athlete and then begin to look for creative ways for God to help us minister to the players in need.

How Do I Cultivate a Growing Relationship with God While Discipling Student-Athletes?

Many times, in talking with athletes about the four areas (academic, athletic, social, and spiritual) of whole-person development, I am asked, "what is the most important relationship?" Without question, the most important relationship an athlete can have is with God. The Godward connection impacts all other relationships in life. Yes, relationships with coaches, teachers and people are very important, however, an athlete's relationship with God is most significant. A growing relationship with God just doesn't happen all by itself. Our heavenly Father always desires a relationship with His children. For the relationship to grow there are some aspects of discipline on the part of the athlete that must be a part of the relationship. To have a healthy growing relationship with God as a student-athlete, the following spiritual disciplines should be integrated into the relationship with God and others; inwardly motivated to match one's talk with one's walk, listening to heathy Christian music, renewing your mind through scripture meditation, consistent study, refection and application of God's Word, regular communication with God through prayer, journaling, accountability with at least one other teammate, and regular

101

fellowship with other believers on the team or outside the sport.

Growing a relationship with God is not about checking off boxes to let others know we have done something, rather it's an inward drive motivated by the Holy Spirit to connect what we must do and be with what God desires to do in us and through us is a big part of developing a vibrant growing relationship with God.

How Do I Maintain Healthy Priorities in the Process of Discipling Student-Athletes?

A question that is raised sometimes by those who are hoping or thinking about going into sport ministry has to do with maintaining proper priorities. It is important to have a few guidelines in place so that one can maintain a good balance in ministry. I have always suggested the following three guidelines in maintaining proper properties as an athlete; *God first…* My relationship with God. If this is the starting point of the day, then one is off to a good start. Making the things of God a top priority helps an athlete develop a good pattern for everyday life. Starting the day off with a God focus is always a good thing. *Family second…* My relationship with my family. If you neglect your family priories you put a strain on the family that can be used by Satan to create confusion in the family. When there is confusion in the family, the enemy is at his best because his goal is to destroy the family. *Ministry third...* My Relationship with those I serve and work with. As I fulfill the first two priorities, I can speak into the lives of those I am working with. Sometimes the priorities get mixed up and difficult decisions must be made that may impact the second and third priority in a negative manner. When something happens that changes those priorities, my encouragement is to ask God for wisdom as you continue to minister to others to the best of your ability under those circumstances and seek godly counsel if needed. The enemy only has one goal in all these areas, to destroy our relationship with God, family and ministry.

Questions to Consider When Discipling Student-Athletes

> *Which Student-Athletes Do I Start the Discipleship Ministry with?*
> *How Should I Respond When an Athlete Displays A Lack of Interest in Discipleship at Times?*
> *What Should I Do When I Don't Have a Spiritual Leader for a Position Group?*
> *How Do I Involve the Coaches and Support Staff In the Discipleship Ministry?*
> *How Do I Deal with Discouragement in Discipleship Ministry?*
> *How Do I Make a Smooth Transition When Changing a Spiritual Leader in a Position Group?*

- ➤ *What Should I Do If I Don't See the Results in My Discipleship Ministry?*
- ➤ *How Do I Help a Spiritual Leader Who Has Failed in One of the Areas of Whole Person Development?*
- ➤ *What Are Some Possible Outcomes from Discipling Student-Athletes?*
- ➤ *How Do I teach Spiritual Minded Athletes to Support What God Is Doing on The Athletic team?*
- ➤ *How Do I Appoint a Spiritual Leader for the Entire Team?*
- ➤ *How Do I Practice the Ministry of Presence with Student-Athletes?*
- ➤ *How Do I Deal with Moments of Doubt When Discipling Student-Athlete's?*
- ➤ *What Are Some Frustrations in Discipling Student-Athletes?*
- ➤ *How Do I Cultivate a Growing Relationship with God While Discilping Student-Athletes?*
- ➤ *How Do I maintain Healthy Priorities in the process of Discipling Student-Athletes?*

Some Things to Ponder:

- ➤ *What Was One Thing I Learned from Reading the Chapter?*
- ➤ *How Will I Apply the One Thing I Have Learned from Reading the Chapter?*

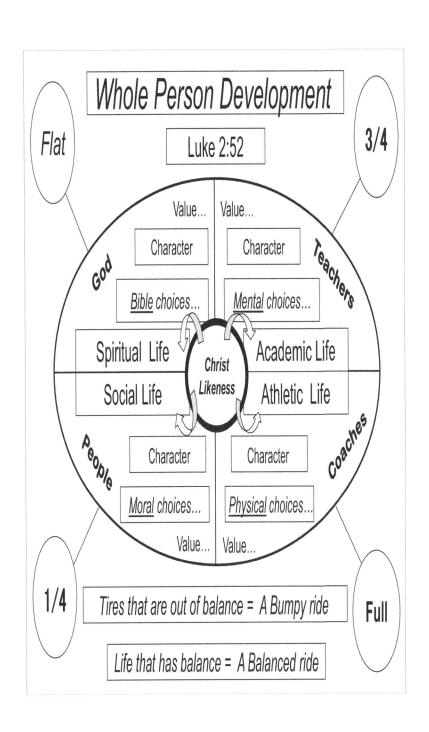

Whole-Person Development Components

Luke 2:52

Athletically

To prepare physically and mentally to compete in competition

Academically

To acquire an education for life after athletics

Socially

To appropriate positive interaction with fellow students, faculty, and community

Spiritually

To foster growth through spiritual and biblical character development

Whole Person Development Questions for Coaches and Leaders to Ask

Questions related to *Athletic* Life

Are you making progress in the weight room?

Who do you hold accountable in the weight room?

Are you getting the proper rest needed to excel?

Are you eating properly?

What are you doing extra to improve your game?

What specific position skills are you working on?

Are you drinking plenty of fluids?

What are your plans for the summer?

What are your physical performance goals?

Are you getting the proper treatment?

Do you have a game plan to meet your athletic goals?

Have you shared your goals with another teammate?

How much time do you spend studying the playbook?

Have you talked to a coach lately?

Are you watching enough film?

Are your goals realistic?

What Character qualities apply here?

Whole Person Development Questions for Coaches and Leaders to Ask

Questions related to *Academic* Life

Are you completing your homework?

Are you using your time wisely?

Do you need help with any classes?

Have you talked with your Advisor?

Are you showing up to class on time?

Do you know your teachers?

Are you sitting in the right seat?

Do you need tutoring in any area?

Is anybody holding you accountable?

When do you plan to graduate?

Is your room clean or messy?

Are you attending all your classes?

How are your grades?

Are you thinking correctly about life?

Do you need to talk to anybody?

Are you utilizing your resources?

What Character qualities apply here?

Whole Person Development Questions for Coaches and Leaders to Ask

Questions related to *Social* Life

Do you have a girl friend or boyfriend?

How long have you been dating?

Do you have a set of practical standards for dating?

Are you making friends on campus?

Are setting a good example for others to follow?

Who are the significant people in your life?

How do you get to meet other people?

Do you know the school's mission statement?

How do you determine who you associate with?

What is your process for making wise decisions?

Who do you talk with when you have a problem?

Have you shared your dating standards with any adult?

Who is holding you accountable socially?

Are you putting yourself in compromising situations?

Are you aware of what a self-report is?

What Character qualities apply here?

Whole Person Development Questions for Coaches and Leaders to Ask

Questions related to *Spiritual* Life

What does it mean to be born again?

Do you attend church anywhere?

What is your religious background?

Is prayer a normal part of your life?

Do you read you bible regularly?

Who are you helping spiritually?

Do you ever doubt your salvation?

Are you accountable spiritually?

How do you determine your identity?

Is there a habit getting you down?

What is your Christian service?

Is anybody helping you spiritually?

How are you encouraging others?

Who do you respect spiritually?

What Character qualities apply here?

Whole Person Development
Questions for Student-Athletes to Ask

Questions related to *Athletic* Life

Am I making progress in the weight room?

Who do I hold accountable in the weight room?

Am I getting the proper rest needed to excel?

Am I eating properly?

What am I doing extra to improve my game?

What specific position skills am I working on?

Am I drinking plenty of fluids?

What are my plans for the summer?

What are my physical performance goals?

Am I getting the proper treatment?

Do I have a game plan to meet my athletic goals?

Have I shared my goals with another teammate?

How much time do I spend studying the playbook?

Have I talked to my position coach lately?

Am I watching enough film?

Are my goals realistic?

What Character qualities apply here?

Whole Person Development Questions for Student-Athletes to Ask

Questions related to *Academic* Life

Am I completing my homework?

Am I using my time wisely?

Do I need help with any classes?

Am I eating properly?

Have I talked with my Advisor?

Am I showing up to class on time?

Do I know my teachers?

Am I sitting in the right seat?

Do I need tutoring in any area?

Is anybody holding me accountable?

When do I plan to graduate?

Is my room clean or messy?

Am I attending all my classes?

How are my grades?

Am I thinking correctly about life?

Do I need to talk to anybody?

Am I utilizing my resources?

What Character qualities apply here?

Whole Person Development
Questions for Student-Athletes to Ask

Questions related to *Social* Life

Do I have a girl friend or boyfriend?

How long have I been dating?

Do I have a set of practical standards for dating?

Am I making friends on campus?

A I setting a good example for others to follow?

Who are the significant people in my life?

How do I get to meet other people?

Do I know the school's mission statement?

How do I determine who I associate with?

What is my process for making wise decisions?

Who do I talk with when I have a problem?

Have I shared my dating standards with any adult?

Who is holding me accountable socially?

Am I putting myself in compromising situations?

Am I aware of what a self-report is?

What Character qualities apply here?

Whole Person Development Questions for Student-Athletes to Ask

Questions related to *Spiritual* Life

What does it mean to be born again?

Do I attend church anywhere?

What is my religious background?

Is prayer a normal part of my life?

Do I read my bible regularly?

Who am I helping spiritually?

Do I ever doubt my salvation?

Am I accountable spiritually?

What is my spiritual game plan?

How do I determine my identity?

Is there a habit getting me down?

Is anybody helping me spiritually?

How am I encouraging others?

Who do I respect spiritually?

What Character qualities apply here?

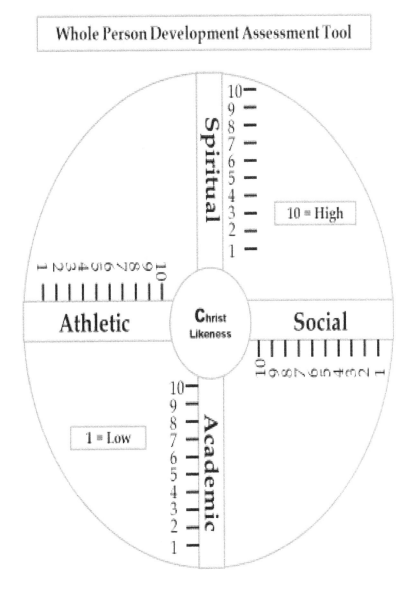

Circle the number that best describes me in each area

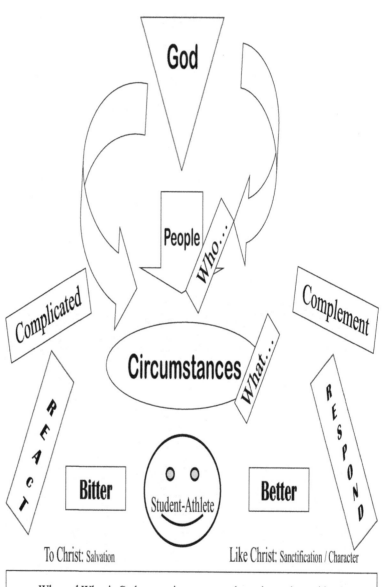

God

People Who...

Complicated   Complement

Circumstances What...

REACT   RESPOND

Bitter   Student-Athlete   Better

To Christ: Salvation   Like Christ: Sanctification / Character

Who and What is God attempting to use to shape the student-athlete?

Character Qualities

ALERTNESS

Being aware of the events taking place around me so that
I can have the right responses to them

ATTENTIVENESS

Showing the worth of a person by giving undivided attention
to their words and emotions

OBEDIENCE

Fulfilling instructions so that the one I am serving will be
fully satisfied and pleased

CONTENTMENT

Realizing that God has provided everything I need for my
present happiness

ORDERLINESS

Learning to organize and care for personal possessions

REVERENCE

Learning to give honor where honor is due and to respect the
possessions and property of others

FORGIVENESS

Clearing the record of those who have wronged me and
not holding their past offenses against them

GRATEFULNESS

Making known in what ways He has benefited my life

FAITH

Developing an unshakable confidence in God
and acting upon it

TRUTHFULNESS

Earning future trust by accurately reporting past facts

SECURITY

Structuring my life around what is eternal and cannot be destroyed or taken away

MEEKNESS

Learning to live with power under control

CAUTIOUSNESS

Seeing future consequences of present actions

PATIENCE

Accepting a difficult situation without demanding a deadline to remove it

DEPENDABILITY

Fulfilling what I consented to do even if it means unexpected sacrifice

DETERMINATION

Purposing to accomplish goals in time regardless of the opposition

PUNCTUALITY

Showing respect for other people and the limited time that they have

DISCERNMENT

The ability to understand why things happen to me and others

LOYALTY

Using difficult times to demonstrate my commitment to others or what is right

COMPASSION

Investing whatever is necessary to heal the hurts of others by the willingness to bear their pain

THRIFTINESS

Not letting myself or others spend that which is not necessary

RESPONSIBILITY

Knowing and doing what is expected from me

VIRTUE

Learning to build personal moral standards which will cause others to desire a more moral life

TOLERANCE

Learning to accept others as a valuable individual regardless of their maturity

FAIRNESS

Looking at a decision from the viewpoint of each person involved

JOYFULNESS

Learning how to lift the spirits and to be pleasant regardless of the outside circumstances

WISDOM

Learning to see and respond to life from another's perspective; the application of knowledge

SELF-CONTROL

Bringing my thoughts, words, actions, and attitudes into constant obedience in order to benefit others

DISCRETION

The ability to avoid words, actions and attitudes which could result in undesirable consequences

DILIGENCE

Visualizing each task as a special assignment and using all my energies to accomplish it

ENDURANCE

The inward strength to withstand stress to manage what occurs in my life

DEFERENCE

Limiting my freedom to speak and act in order not to offend the tastes of others

SINCERITY

Eagerness to do what is right without ulterior motives

GENEROSITY

Realizing that all I have belongs to God and freely giving of these to benefit others

HUMILITY

Seeing the contrast between what is perfect and my inability to achieve it

ENTHUSIASM

Learning what actions and attitudes please others and becoming excited about doing them

INITIATIVE

Recognizing and doing what needs to be done before I am asked to do it

LOVE

Learning to serve the basic needs of others without motive or personal reward

CREATIVITY

Applying wisdom and practical insights to a need or task

DECISIVENESS

Learning to finalize difficult decisions on the basis of what is right

SENSITIVITY

Knowing what words and actions will benefit others

THOROUGHNESS

Realizing that each of our tasks will be reviewed

RESOURCEFULNESS

Wise use of that which others would normally overlook or discard

FLEXIBILITY

Learning how to cheerfully change plans when unexpected conditions require it

AVAILABILITY

Making my own schedule and priorities secondary to the wishes of those I am serving

HOSPITALITY

Cheerfully sharing food, shelter, and my life with those whom I come in contact

GENTLENESS

Learning to respond to needs with kindness, personal care, and love

BOLDNESS

Demonstrating the confidence that doing what is right
will bring ultimate victory regardless
of present opposition

PERSUASIVENESS

Using words which cause the listener's spirit to confirm
that he is hearing truth

COURAGE

Fulfilling my responsibilities in spite of being afraid

Used by permission from Character That Counts / Rod Handley

How to Respond to People and Situations with Character?

What can I learn about God from the person or situation?

Make a list of what was learned about God

What can I learn about myself through the person and situation?

Make a list of what I learned about myself

What character qualities apply to the situation?

Check off the character qualities that apply to the situation
Write out one-character quality on a card to begin to work on
Begin to memorize, apply and review character quality

What can I learn about the person?

Make a list of what was learned about the person
Attempt to attach new meaning to the person
Attempt to attach new meaning to the way I think about the person

What do I need to think about before attempting to communicate?

Is it the Right Place?
Is it the Right Time?
Do I have the Right Attitude?
Have I selected the Right Words?
Have I thought through the questions to ask?

First Category of Student-Athletes –

High Interest Group

Intentional about Cultivating Their Relationship with God

and Impacting Others

Characteristics of Student-Athletes in High-Interest Group

- Consistent intake and application of God's Word
- Focused prayer time
- Attempts to help others grow spiritually
- Has an awareness of God in daily life
- May attend a local church or on-campus church
- Attempts to live out the mission of the school
- Inwardly motivated to grow spiritually
- Experiences normal struggles in daily walk
- Light and Salt to others
- Sometimes not the most vocal group player on the team
- May assume a spiritual leadership position in another area at school or at local church
- A good example for others to follow
- Sometimes not the most talented player on the team

Reflections of High-Interest Group to Others

- A desire to cultivate relations with God and impact teammates
- Individual commitment to Whole-Person Development
- Interest in spiritual things
- A positive influence on others
- Developing an eternal value system
- May have been discipled by someone else

Reasons for Being Placed in the High-Interest Group

- Has been born again
- Is intentional about cultivating relationship with God
- Has a desire to develop biblical value system
- Has a desire to live out the reality of God in front of others
- Has a desire to help others grow
- Has an interest in utilizing spiritual disciplines in personal life

Second Category of Student-Athletes –

Some Interest Group

Could be a new Christian or someone who is saved but life is still all about self

Characteristics of Student-Athletes in Some-Interest Group

- Spiritual Disciplines not a top priority

- Temporal things have a tendency to supersede spiritual things
- Lives life with a "take it or leave it" approach to spiritual disciplines
- Certain events at certain times may trigger a spiritual interest
- No consistent plan for spiritual growth
- A hit or miss approach to spiritual things
- Worldly things overshadow spiritual things in life
- Fear of what others may think

Reflections of Some-Interest Group to Others

- Minimal interest in spiritual things / Spiritual infancy
- Spiritual values are not a priority in daily life
- No enthusiasm for spiritual things
- Little influence spiritually on others
- May have never been discipled by someone else

Reasons for being placed in the Some-Interest Group

- Lack of spiritual consecration
- Temporary value system
- Past failure
- Possible personal defeat in daily life
- Possible wrong thought patterns about God, self and others

Third Category of Student-Athletes –

No Interest Group

Maybe interested in spiritual things, but has not given a clear cut testimony of salvation

Characteristics of Student-Athletes in No-Interest Group

- Never been born again
- No interest in spiritual things
- No interest in attending the local church
- Over emphasis on self
- No conscious awareness of God in the daily things of life
- Spiritual disciplines are more academic than life-changing

Reflections of No-Interest Group to Others

- Never born again
- No interest in spiritual things
- No spiritual life
- No spiritual influence on others

Reasons for being placed in the No-Interest Group

- Never born again
- No outward evidence of genuine conversation

SPIRITUAL – ASSESSMENT QUESTIONNAIRE

Print Clearly

Print Name _____   _____

Date _____

*Answer **honestly** by circling the most appropriate circle that best describes me right now*

Do I <u>know</u> I am Christian?

- o I know for sure I am a Christian
- o I am not sure I am a Christian
- o I would like to know for sure I am a Christian

Do I <u>attend</u> church while in college?

- o Not at all
- o Once in awhile
- o On a regular basis

Do I <u>read</u> my Bible?

- o Sometimes
- o Not at all
- o Regularly

Do I have a <u>desire</u> to grow in my relationship with God?

- o No desire at this time
- o A little desire
- o A very high desire

Do I have some <u>idea</u> about what I want to do after graduation?

      o No idea
      o Some idea
      o Have a good idea

Do I have <u>something</u> I need to talk with someone about?

      o Not at this time
      o Yes I do

Dorm and Room Number: _____ Cell Phone

Number: _____

Position: _____ Birthday _____ _____

Maximizing the Whole Person Development Model

How Can The Whole Person Development Model Be Utilized?

When dealing with an in sport or off sport event issue

When talking with parents and potential student-athletes during a recruiting presentation

When talking with a student-athlete about adding value to the athletic program

When talking with someone outside the athletic program

When talking to or about another athletic team

When talking with athletic and academic administrators

How Can Athletics Utilize The Whole Person Development Model?

When talking about athletics to the general public

When talking with potential staff members

When attending conferences

When talking with potential student-athletes

When talking with parents of potential student-athletes

When talking with student-athletes

How Can Coaches/Support Staff Use The Whole Person Development model?

When talking one on one with student-athletes

When talking to coaches on the road while recruiting

When talking with parents and potential student-athletes

When talking with players about adding value to the football program

When talking with players in their position groups

When engaged in the evaluation process of student-athletes

Notes

Chapter One: Why Should Student Athletes Be Discipled?
1. Billie Hanks Jr., Discipleship, Zondervan, Page 20
2. Tony Dungy, Mentor Leaders, Tyndale House Publisher, Page 7
3. Bill Gothard, Basic Institute of Conflicts, C.W. Post College, 1973
4. Martin Sanders, The Power of Mentoring, Page 64
5. Gary Kuhue, The Dynamics of Discipleship Training, Zondervan, Page 14

Chapter Two: When Should Student Athletes Be Discipled?
1. Bruce Wilkerson, Secrets of the Vine, Multnomah Publishers, Page 46
2. Dennis Maynard, Pastoral Counseling, McNaughton and Gunn, Page Unknown

Chapter Three: Where Should Student Athletes Be Discipled?
1. Dave Early, Leading Small Groups, Touch Publishers, Page 13
2. David Stoddard, The Heart of Mentoring, NavPress, Page 109
3. Tim Elmore, Life Giving Mentors, Growing Leaders, Page 15

Chapter Four: How Should Student Athletes Be Discipled?
1. Joel Manby, Love Works, Zondervan, Page 115
2. Tim Clinton, Turn Your Life Around, Faith Works, Page 198
3. Chris Adsit, Personal Disciplemaking, Campus Crusade for Christ, Page 53

Chapter Five: What Areas Should Student Athletes Be
   Discipled In?
   1.   Patrick Morley, A Man's Guide Spiritual Disciplines,
   Page 16
   2.   Terry Wardle, The Transforming Path, Leafwood
   Publishers, Page 58
   3.   Jon Gordon, The Power of Positive Team, Wiley
   Publishers, Page 47
   4.   John Maxwell, Leadershift, Harper Collins, Page 134
   5.   Kenneth Boa, Conformed To His Image, Zondervan,
   Page 101
   6.   Jeff Janssen, Team Captains Leadership Manual,
   Winning the Mental Game, Page xz
   7.   Dallas Willard, The Revolution of Character,
   NavPress, Page 115
   8.   Bill Hybel's, Who You Are When No One Is
   Looking, Inter-Varsity Press, Page 9

Chapter Six: Who Should Disciple Student Athletes?
   1.   John Ortburg, The Power of One on One, Baker
   Books, Page 11
   2.   Jim Stump, The Power of One of One, Baker Books,
   Page 25

Chapter Seven: Things to Remember When Discipling
   Students Athletes
   1.   Tim Tebow, Through My Eyes, Harper Collins
   Publisher, Page x
   2.   Andy Stanley, The Next Generation Leader,
   Multnomah Publishers, Page 106
   3.   James Kouzes, Leadership Challenge, Jossey Bass
   Publishers, Page 120

4.   Rod Dempsey, Leading A Small Group, Touch Publishers, Page 228

Chapter Eight: The Nuts and Bolts for Effective Discipleship Ministry
1.   Ed Gomes
2.   Barry Black, The Blessing of Adversity, Tyndale Publishers, Page 67
3.   Mel Lawrenze, Patterns, Zondervan, Page 67

Chapter Nine: Questions to Consider When Discipling Student Athletes
1.   Clay Scroggins, How To Lead When You are Not In Charge, Zondervan, Page 45
2.   Bill Hybels, Courageous leadership, Zondervan, Page 122
3.   Bob Reccord, Beneath The Surface, Broadman Publishers, Page 34
4.   Greg Ogden, Transforming Discipleship, Inter Varsity Press, Page 103
5.   Manual Chavier, International Church of the Nazarene, 1990

Made in the USA
Monee, IL
25 August 2021

75899828R00080